ase return / renew by date shown.

LOUISE OF SARNIA

LOUISE OF SARNIA

Wallis Peel

CHIVERS

British Library Cataloguing in Publication Data available

This Large Print edition published by AudioGO Ltd, Bath, 2012.
Published by arrangement with the Author

U.K. Hardcover   ISBN 978 1 4713 1335 6
U.K. Softcover   ISBN 978 1 4713 1336 3

Printed and bound in Great Britain by
MPG Books Group Limited

For Jane Tatam of Amolibros

Sarnia is the true name of Guernsey from the traditional Latin. 'Sarnia Cherie' is the title of the island's national anthem, with its delightful and eloquent words. A pleasure to read—and sing.

Who never has suffered, he has lived but
    half
Who never failed, he never strove or sought
Who never wept is stranger to a laugh
And he who never doubted never thought

Rev J B Goode (Ideals Publishing Corp, USA,
    vol 31, no 5, September MCMLXXIV)

AUTHOR'S NOTE

BENSON'S QUARRY is fictitious and has no connection, present or past, with any quarry on any of the Channel Islands.

ONE

1868, Guernsey—Sarnia

The wind howled and made heavy raindrops rattle against the windows. Neither of them was aware of this, both too angry with each other. They glowered and paused to collect their thoughts.

'You can be the most obnoxious daughter anyone could be lumbered with!' Anne Penford snapped, raising herself as tall as possible but aware she lacked Louise's stature. Her cheeks flamed red with temper, her large breasts heaved and she itched to lash out with her right hand.

Louise snorted. 'You're not exactly full of motherly devotion. You never have been. It's always been darling-David-this then dear-David-that, as if he's the be all and end all of life!'

'Well what else do you expect! He's the firstborn and a son!'

'Piffle, Mother!' Louise hurled back. 'He's a spiteful, conniving bully. Look at how he treats Simon, when me and Father are not around!'

'He is not! He just tries to put a bit of backbone into Simon. He's two years younger than you yet often acts like a six-yearold.'

Louise knew what she meant. Her younger brother was backward. He lacked all confidence, which was hardly surprising when

1

bullied so by brother David.Yet she loved him dearly and would fight for him. David was taller and stronger than either of his siblings but he had learned to be very careful of his sister. Louise was perfectly capable of turning on him physically, as she had proved, having once left him with a real black eye.

'Dear David is a nasty piece of work and I predict he'll cause trouble to this family one day!' she snapped.

'Rubbish!' Anne retorted. 'You've always been jealous of him and the fact this house will be his one day—and that's not so far off either.'

Louise caught her breath with frustration. What her mother had said was accurate. She acknowledged the main property always went to the firstborn son, it was their Guernsey law. Yet David did not give a damn about the house, which she adored. It was a solid structure built with taste, with five windows upstairs, as all good houses had. Then her mother's words registered and she frowned with confusion. She stood tall and straight, her hair loosely curled, hanging just above her shoulders. Her eyes were neither blue nor brown, but an attractive hazel colour. This went well with regular features. She had often studied herself in her mirror. She was not beautiful, that she acknowledged, yet she thought perhaps she did have a little something unusual. She was correct. Her

2

strong spirit blazed like a beacon. Physical beauty was irrelevant.

'What exactly do you mean, Mother? Not so far off?' she cried and frowned.

'Exactly what I say. We're moving into town and about time too. I'm sick of being stuck here at Cobo. At least in St Peter Port there'll be some life. A few decent people around, more activity. David will take the house ready for when he marries!'

Louise was shocked and lost for words momentarily. This had not entered her head. If only her father was not away so much, doing— what, she asked herself? Then her bright mind replied. She had a shrewd idea how he filled in his days and was now desperate to talk to him.

'Where is Father?' she managed to get out at last.

Her mother threw a noncommittal shrug of genuine disinterest. 'Who knows or cares, not me!'

'But you don't mind the money he brings in though, do you, Mother!' Louise threw at her.

'That's his job to provide and that's another thing. It's high time you were wed. Look at you! Nearly eighteen years, spending your days nose stuck in books. High time you ran your own home with one on the way!'

'Don't start and be crude, Mother! Such language won't go down well in town!'

'And don't you be sarcastic to me!' and Anne Penford stepped forward briskly. With

3

a speed that surprised even her, she slapped her daughter harshly across her left cheek. Her strong spirit blazed like a beacon.

Louise reeled with shock then her temper rose. Months, perhaps even years of resentment, sheeted high and exploded. She balled her right fist and punched out. More by luck than any judgement her fist connected flush on her mother's chin. Anne Penford went flying backwards, totally unbalanced and crashed to the carpet, skirt riding high, displaying long pink bloomers.

'Why you misbegotten hussy—how dare you!' she screeched. 'Strike your own mother!'

'Serve you right!' Louise shouted back, rather astonished with herself, but not at all sorry. This had been coming on for ages, she realised.

The lounge door banged open suddenly. 'What the hell is going on here? I could hear the pair of you outside. Sounded like a couple of alley cats!' Danny Penford grated as he quickly took in the whole scene. He tossed off his sodden cape, shook water from his drenched hair and gritted his teeth.

'She punched me!' Anne screamed again. 'Her own mother!'

'She started it, Father!' Louise bellowed back, teeth set, temper very high now.

'As her mother I've the right to discipline her because you let her do just as she likes!'

Danny stifled a groan and gave a tiny shake

4

of his head. What the devil had he ever seen in this woman he'd married? Talk about marry in haste to repent in leisure! Thank heavens he had it within his power to change this situation even if at a price. He flashed a look at Louise, whom, secretly, he adored. Then he nodded upwards and she received the message with the natural rapport between them. She spun on her heel and left the large sitting room.

'You have only yourself to blame, wife,' Danny grated. 'Now get up, stop showing off your drawers and simmer down. Louise has spirit, more than the boys put together.'

'She's rabid with jealousy over dear David, especially as she now knows we're moving and the house will be his. Why she's always made such an ado about this place is beyond me,' she said, standing, pulling down her skirt and rubbing what would be a very sore jaw. 'I want her out of the home.' She almost spat out the words. 'Get her married or do something but I'll not live in any town house with her!'

Danny said nothing, but his mind raced. This situation could be providential to his plans. 'I'll consider the matter,' he said slowly, picking up his still sodden waterproof, then leaving the room he went to look for Louise.

She was in her room. Louise eyed her father a bit dubiously. She realised she had done wrong through constant provocation. She tried to read her father as he stepped in, looked around but said nothing for a few moments.

5

It was a generous sized room, kept beautifully tidy and neat with books everywhere, especially on her little desk. He studied the only two pictures that, long ago, he had given to his girl. One showed violent rough seas with swirling colours of greys and light blues, which gently floated into each other. The second was another one of his selections. It showed a large clipper coming into the harbour at St Peter Port, people waiting to board, carriers standing by to unload. It was a pure action picture. He lifted each down, carefully studied their backs, then he re-hung them, watched by a puzzled daughter.

'I need to have a long talk with you,' he began carefully. 'Tomorrow I'm sailing. I want you with me because you don't get seasick, do you?'

Louise shook her head firmly. 'No, Pa,' and she could not resist the next few words. 'Unlike David!'

Danny Penford turned and faced her four square. He was a tall man, well over six feet with broad shoulders and not an ounce of fat on him. He usually kept his face well shaved unless he'd been at sea and, Louise knew, this now explained the generous shadow of black whiskers. She considered him very good looking and was honest enough to admit to herself he had become her benchmark where young males were concerned.

'You certainly can't stand your elder

brother, can you?' he asked quietly.

Louise was well known for being forthright. 'I loathe him and as to him having this house—' She waved a hand in a helpless gesture of disapproval. 'It's all just bricks and mortar to him. To me,' and she lifted her hand once more, 'it's a darling place!'

He understood her better than she realised. 'That's as maybe. It's his and he needs it now he's getting married. Anyhow your mother has always hated Cobo since she set foot here. Perhaps she might just be sweeter-tempered in town with people around her for socialising. I've bought a decent town house but think you'd be better off away from her, so have arranged a place for you at St Sampsons until you wed,' he informed her carefully, and awaited her reaction.

'Wed?' Louise gasped.

'Yes! You and Simon can lodge in a decent apartment with someone to look after you until you marry.'

He took a deep breath and came out with it: 'Jack Noyen has spoken to me about you. He really fancies you and he's a pretty good bloke all round. A very sound fisherman with his own smack and crew. You'd never want with him and he's not bad-looking either.'

'Well!' was all Louise could manage, as her mind revolved. She knew Noyen a little but suddenly felt she was being stampeded, and her teeth clenched. 'As the female I'm the one

7

to say yes or no, Pa!' and she snorted. 'I'm not in all that much of a rush to start producing and to hell with what Mother thinks!'

Danny had empathy for her and sufficient knowledge of her character not to try and force an issue. This girl of his, 'the best one I bred' he told himself, must be amenable. She was quite correct about his firstborn, and the last one, Simon, was lacking where brains were concerned, though gentle and harmless with his failing. Louise was tough and he knew, upon her would depend the family position and future if anything happened to him.

'Okay!' he drawled in a noncommittal voice, which did not fool Louise with one syllable.

'You're up to something, Pa,' she accused calmly while her mind raced.

'Who, me?' he asked innocently, then chuckled. 'Let's say I've a lot to discuss with you when we're alone without interruptions from anyone,' he explained slowly. 'I've a new ketch and we'll sail off in her for a few days. I'll take those two pictures with me and see they're hung in your apartment for when you return. Your mother can do her own thing arranging to move. Just you pack up your personal things today and I'll see some are moved right away.' He paused. 'Noyen is going to help. Coming over with a box cart early this evening.'

Louise frowned at that. She felt she was being pushed, too far and too fast. She scowled. Danny grinned at this sudden pugnacity but thoroughly approved her spirit.

'He won't bite!' he teased.

'Pa!' she protested, then felt her own lips twitch. 'In that case you'd better let me start to pack, but you hear me, Pa,' and her voice sank as she faced him grimly. 'I don't know how it will happen or even when but this I do know. One day this house will be mine. Mine! All mine!'

He did not reply. He had no words to satisfy her. Everyone was entitled to hold to a dream, and if this was what his girl thought and wished he could not disabuse her. By his logic what she wanted was an impossibility, unless—and a thought shot into his head. What if David only spawned girls? He threw her a thoughtful look, took her two cherished pictures under one arm, opened the door and left her to it, but walked straight into his son and heir.

'I presume you know what's going to happen?' he barked.

David Penford was afraid of his father, as he had also learned to be wary of his sister. 'Yes, sir,' he said quickly.

'In that case leave your sister and Simon alone or I'll see you attend your wedding with two black eyes,' he snapped coldly, then turned abruptly on his heel and strode away, mind buzzing with all kinds of possibilities.

David eyed him and cursed silently but knew better than to disobey. He'd tell his one great ally about it all. His mother. Thank God Louise and Simon were going to live elsewhere and he'd have the house to himself and his bride. He thundered down the stairs, almost but not quite a replica of his sire, being shorter, while his looks lacked his father's ruggedness and the skin colouring got from the sea breezes. David did not like the sea one iota. It was inclined to move about too much for his queasy stomach. He was a pure landsman.

Left alone, Louise moved around automatically, her mind buzzing. Jack Noyen? Well, should she encourage him or be standoffish? She knew him a little. He was a couple of years older and came from a hardworking fishing family, theirs a valued and respected island occupation. There was good money in fishing but also danger. Many smacks had gone down in sudden storms with precious few crew surviving.

There had been plenty of other young males who had hopefully set their caps at her, encouraged by her mother, to get her out of the home. But Jack Noyen? Where was this apartment to be? All of a sudden she realised her father had given her but bare bones. He *was* up to something and she itched now to know what.

She worked rapidly, throwing clothes into baskets and wrapping in sheets other personal items. When laboriously trundling them to the back door, a box cart drew up with Jack Noyen grinning at her.

'Hello, Louise. All ready for me?' he chuckled, delighted to see her alone at last but uncertain as to the best way to approach her. Danny Penford had warned she had strong opinions and a temper when provoked. 'Here, let me sling everything up. Any breakables in this lot?'

Louise shook her head and eyed him carefully. He was good looking in a way with a nice manner—but marry him? That could be a step much too far. 'Where am I going?'

'Didn't your father explain? You're going to stay with one of my aunts. She is a widow and lives in a largish house and will be glad to have company. Not far from St Sampsons. Easy to drive into town yet away from all the bustle,' he explained.

Louise shook her head with exasperation at her father and his schemes, then she slowly accepted she would learn much more when they were alone, away from this darling house.

Jack eyed her stance, which was almost aloof, and knew he must say something. She was such a splendid girl and would make an ideal mate, but how best to approach her? He plunged wildly.

'Your old man said you might help me—' He paused. Now he had her attention.

'Doing what?' Louise asked suspiciously, her mind racing once more.

11

'My books!'

Louise blinked. 'Books?'

'No, not the novel type. My account books, which are in a bit of a mess,' he explained hopefully. 'I desperately need someone to straighten them out and keep them up to date. What profit can I expect when I've sold at the market and paid my crew? I always add a percentage bonus for my men,' he told her.

She studied him carefully. He was good-looking in a rugged way without being flashy. His skin weather-beaten but clean-shaven. He wore a loose muffler tossed around his neck, over his jacket. He wore thick seamen's trousers and solid ankle boots. He looked reliable.

Figures were fun to Louise and she knew she was interested. What was this about living with one of his relatives? Once more she felt as if she were being pushed forward much too fast and she instinctively dug in her heels. 'I'll think it over,' she prevaricated.

He pulled a face but had sense enough not to push. Not yet, anyway.

'You'll like my Aunt Janet,' he told her. As she climbed up on the seat with him he picked up the reins and clucked at the horse to move off.

When she passed no comment he racked his brains for intelligent conversation. 'I don't know your brother Simon very well,' he began again. 'Though I know David better but

. . .' and now his words tailed off. He cursed silently to himself. Where was the necessary sparkling conversation?

'And?' Louise almost barked at him.

He was startled and flashed a look at her face, with jaw now set grimly. He remembered what her old man had said. No love lost between this brother and sister. 'Fancies himself, doesn't he?' then paused to add, 'Not my type at all.'

Louise gazed frankly. 'I loathe him,' she explained, 'and it's mutual. Simon is fine. Not at all bright upstairs but good with his hands if given half a chance,' she added gently.

He was suddenly genuinely interested. 'Is that so? Maybe he can help me on my fishing smack. There always seem jobs to do, make-and-mend-type, and I never get around to them. Do you think he'd come aboard and look around for me?'

Louise threw him her first genuine smile. 'I'm sure he would. How long has your aunt been widowed? How come my pa knows her?' she shot at him as a new thought slipped into her mind. She was under no illusions, her parents did not get on at all and a move into town would hardly change their situation. Did her pa also have a 'lady' friend? She itched to know but, if he did, she would never blame him. Whatever there might have been in their early married days had long vanished, starting with the birth of David—her mother's new toy,

13

which even her birth and that of Simon later had never changed. Good luck to him, she mused. She didn't blame him at all and now looked forward keenly to meeting this aunt of Jack's.

'Not much further to go. I'll introduce you, get your gear in the room aunt will have selected, then go back for Simon and his stuff. Your pa said you'd be going away with him for a couple of days or so. When you come back you can settle in with Aunty and hopefully you'll help me. I'm a good fisherman but I'd never make an accountant,' he told her with a grimace. She certainly was no chatterbox! 'Here we are!' and he pulled up the box cart, sprang down and went to help her, but Louise swung her long skirt aside and jumped down nimbly as the front door opened.

'Jack—and you must be Louise! Welcome! It's going to be wonderful to have company!'

Louise stared and took her all in. Possibly in her early forties. Not tall, big bosomed with a cheerful face, beaming a smile of genuine delight. 'Your father was here earlier on. He hung two of your pictures in what will be your room! I hope you'll like it. It gets the early morning sun and the room opposite will be for your brother,' she explained, and grasping her hand took Louise indoors.

It was not a large house, unlike that she'd left at Cobo, but it had a good atmosphere. It was spotlessly clean and as she went up the stairs Louise knew right away she could be happy here—for the time being. Her room was smaller than before and started to fill up as Jack brought up her possessions. She spotted her two pictures and Louise smiled. The sight of them stamped her persona on the room.

'Will this do?'

Louise faced her and smiled. 'It's quite delightful!' she replied, and meant it. The older woman opened a facing door.'For your brother,' and Louise stepped in. It was not quite as large as her room but would be ideal for Simon and his quiet ways.

'I'll provide all your meals. Your father has arranged this with me.'

'Have you known him long, Janet?—I presume it's okay to call you that?'

Janet had been ready for the question. 'Of course I'm Janet,' she said reassuringly 'I've been friends with your father for a few years. He knew my late husband. He died a year or so ago, leaving me this house. It was a heart attack and so sudden. Your father was very kind to me,' she explained slowly. 'And we just became good friends.'

Louise had enough sense and tact to question no more, though she knew, later on, her mind would work fast. If there was anything going on between Janet and her father, that was their business. Not hers. Then she tilted her head.

'I could have sworn I heard a pigeon

cooing!'

'Quite likely. My husband kept two or three and it seems they like it in the loft!' and she nodded above her head to where a trapdoor nestled in the ceiling. 'Must go and give them some corn!'

Louise let her gaze roam her room. A good single bed, a wardrobe and chest of drawers and she decided her desk could stand next to it. She eyed a pile of her possessions, just dropped down by Jack who had departed for Simon's goods. With gusto she attacked the myriad bundles, and in a delightfully short time had a semblance of order in her new room. Janet appeared suddenly with a steaming mug of tea.

'My! That didn't take you long. I can see grass isn't allowed to grow under your feet!' she praised with a chuckle. 'Will Simon move in today as well?'

Louise pulled a face then nodded. 'He'll be glad to,' she explained, wondering exactly what details her father had given to his friend. How much of a proper 'friend' was Janet? It made an intriguing question, which only her father could answer.

It was the first night she'd ever spent in strange surroundings, yet she slept well. Simon had appeared much later and Jack had buckled to in order to help him unpack, then with a cheerful nod had departed. It was Janet who'd explained he still lived at home with his

16

parents. 'He wants his own place, that I know, but—' and Janet did not finish her sentence, which was not missed by Louise. She finally fell asleep with a buzzing mind.

It was Simon who tapped on her door in the morning. 'Hi, sis!' and he grinned. He was of average height with curled hair a bit dark like hers, and fair features. His was a happy-go-lucky nature with most people, but he was afraid of his brother David. He always had been. His wonderful sister was his champion and he adored her for it. She was two years older and always so reliable and quite capable of flying at David when he was in a bullying mood, which, to Simon, was always when he was unfortunate enough to be around. Now he was to live here, away from big brother bully David. It had all happened so swiftly and he was overjoyed.

'Happy now?' Louise asked him gently.

'It's wonderful. Now I want to leave schooling behind to make my life perfect,' he confided.

Louise had already worked that one out. 'Leave it to Pa,' she advised. 'He'll sort something out,' she predicted.

'Though I don't know exactly what I can do,' Simon admitted slowly. 'I'm not clever like you or David,' and his voice had a sorrowful tone.

It was Janet who provided an instant occupation. 'Simon, your father wants you to drive your sister down to the town harbour to meet him, then come back and take me shopping. I have a paddock at the rear with a pony and you'll find the trap near the gate,' she explained.

'But where at the harbour?' Louise queried. 'It's a big place and always so busy!'

Janet turned to her. 'He'll be on the lookout for you,' and she paused a moment. 'He said straight after breakfast because of the tide.'

'In that case we'd better get moving,' Louise said practically. 'Off you go, Simon, and when I do get back we'll have a good old chat,' she promised, 'so don't fret about anything!'

*   *   *

As Simon drove the trap away Louise stood uncertainly. There was so much activity. The harbour was just about full and the quayside the same, thronged with people. Passengers waiting to board and sail over to England. Many men were waiting to unload new arrivals and load others on their way out. She was so engrossed she jumped when a hand clapped her shoulder.

'Glad you're on time!' Danny told her and threw her one of his facetious grins. 'I've a new ketch!' and he pointed to one side.

Louise was taken aback. 'She is so small,' she gasped. 'Can't carry many goods for smuggling in her!' Then she realised what she'd blurted out.

'And what exactly do you mean by that, daughter?' Danny barked at her with a stern, almost frigid look.

Louise knew she blushed. 'Well, don't you, Pa? Just about everyone else on this island does. Indeed from bits I've heard in the past it's been big business, especially slipping brandy over to England!'

He gave a grunt that could have meant anything. 'Well if you know so much—there's nothing private in Guernsey, is there? Those days though have just about gone forever. The English have really tightened up their Customs and Excise patrols. Now it's become a dangerous game with shots fired on both sides. Court trials, prison sentences and killings,' he added.

Louise eyed him. He had never lied to her before. Always he had simply refused to answer a difficult question, so why did he sail over to England so much if it wasn't to smuggle brandy? She gave a sigh of exasperation and frustration. He would tell her when he was good and ready and not before.

'She's small for two reasons. She is very fast and I can handle her without a crew. Just someone at the wheel to keep to the heading I give, and that will be you on the way out, but always wear a lifeline,' he said warningly. 'I do. Remember,' and he nodded at the small ketch tied to the harbour below them, 'no brakes! You go overboard and I can't stop in a hurry

19

to rescue you! You hear me, girl!' he growled.

Louise nodded and waved her hand. 'So many people here!'

'True!' he agreed. 'That's why the new harbour is being built, but it'll take time. They started it when you were small. St Julian's Pier is being extended, which will make life easier, not just for passengers but for goods coming and going. This, the castle breakwater and lighthouse, will make such a difference to life here. Look at all the box carts waiting,' and now he pointed. 'Those to unload stone and our island goods, others empty to fill up. Remember, all the anthracite comes in here and that's a rotten job. Loading it into baskets, carrying it up onto the pier and tipping it in the empty box carts. One day there'll be steamers here as well,' he predicted, then looked down at his little ketch and eyed her long skirt. Female clothing was impractical for sailing ships, he considered.

Louise read his mind. 'It's a divided skirt,' she assured him. 'Trousers like men wear would be even better but the old fuddy-duddies like Mother would throw a fit,' and she gave a giggle.

He agreed then became serious. 'Simon?' he asked quietly.

'Different person away from Mother and that David, but he's fed up with schooling.'

'I'm ahead of you there. I've taken him from school and arranged a little job for him at one of the quarries!' he told her.

Louise was startled. 'Simon—a quarry worker, Pa!' she protested almost with horror etched in her voice.

'Relax, girl!' he told her quickly, noting how her jaw had set in a rigid line. He knew she was perfectly capable of squaring up to him. 'It's with horses. He's good with animals and he'll start off working under the stud groom, until he learns enough, then it'll be up to him how far or high he wishes to go!'

'Oh!' she gasped. 'What a good idea!' she praised and he felt himself feeling smug. A compliment from his girl was worth cherishing.

'Yes,' he told himself, 'I have been right with my plans. What a magnificent family matriarch Louise will make.' Then he added aloud, 'David will continue to work in a financial office. It appears they quite like him at his firm!'

Louise let out one of her famous disparaging snorts. 'They may change their mind if he starts to lord it over them. Poor fools!'

'Enough! Time to board. I'll go down the ladder first,' he said changing the subject, because Louise could be vitriolic without much reason where his firstborn was concerned. He swung over the harbour wall and nimbly shot down the short ladder to land lightly on the balls of his feet and watch her follow. She neither hesitated nor put a foot wrong. His heart swelled with pride for his girl.

'We'll go out with the tide, I'll take the con then you can take over while I run up a sail,' and he cast a knowing eye at the sky, noting some clouds building up, and using his experience in calculating the wind. 'We might get some unwelcome pongs near Lithou,' he warned her. 'Burning off the dried seaweed ready to have it made into iodine.'

Louise crinkled her forehead with a gentle frown of interest. 'I've never been there. Silly when I'm an island girl!' she told him.

'Bit different there now to when there was the Priory of Our Lady of Lithou. Now they rake up the vraic and once it's dried it's burned off in a brick-lined pit and the ashes are ready to be processed into iodine,' he explained to her, steering his tiny ketch from the harbour into the open sea.

Louise turned this over in her mind. Iodine from seaweed? It seemed illogical yet she knew it was big business.

TWO

The Little ketch dipped her prow as she met the open water, rather like a curtsey, Louise thought, and she grinned to herself. She then started to scud along briskly.

She watched her father raise one sail then

stroll back to her. 'I'll take her now. Go down to the galley. There's bread and cold meat for sandwiches and I'm peckish!' he said firmly.

Louise threw him a grin and disappeared below. It was all so small to her after his previous ketch but neat and tidy. Dan was left with his thoughts as he sailed on, eyes constantly on the alert. When she appeared with hefty sandwiches he tucked in and eyed her. 'And what exactly do you know about smuggling?'

Louise laughed. 'Enough to know it's been lucrative for many on our island and for umpteen people in England too!'

He nodded. 'As I mentioned before, those days are well and truly gone. New legislation in Guernsey as well as England. It's a dangerous occupation with very alert Customs and Revenue men.'

'But you still do it, Pa!' she replied soberly.

He sniffed and then nodded to one side. 'Lithou, they're burning off!'

Louise sniffed, pulled a face then eyed him. 'Where are we going and for what, Pa? Not much room below to smuggle anything.'

'My cargo has just two legs,' he replied bluntly, 'and you will keep your mouth shut tight. No questions, no nothing. We're heading for Durdle Door, not that far from Melcombe Regis. What makes that place famous or notorious?' he shot at her suddenly.

Louise blinked, baffled, shook her head and

23

waited expectantly.

He grinned down at her as his ketch sailed along briskly but quite gently. 'It's the place in England in 1348 that started the bubonic plague. Came ashore there from a ship and spread like wildfire throughout the land. Now that's a titbit for those young children you teach, though perhaps not. Too young for morbid details like fleas living on *Rattus rattus* and the end result. You're wasting your time at that work. You'd find it much more interesting working for Noyen.'

'You're matchmaking again, Pa!' Louise accused.

'Of course!' he agreed swiftly. 'I've settled your mother in her town house and I predict she'll thrive because she's a social climber. She'll be delighted to live at Hauteville now. Victor Hugo is there, though it's hardly likely he will notice her existence. Too busy writing those books of his, but she'll be flattered to breathe the same air,' he stated sarcastically.

'Did you fall head over heels in love with Mother?' Louise had to ask at last, something she'd pondered for years.

He let out a snort of self-derision. 'I was young, stupid and callow when I lived in England, at Bristol. I felt pity for her. The youngest of a batch of daughters, so little dowry left for her. I think her father was glad to see her settled and I thought a splendid house at Cobo would please her. She started

24

complaining about the isolation after David's birth and never stopped. Perhaps one day—' and he let the sentence hang.

Louise felt pity for him and vowed she'd not make such a mistake, but was he right about working for Noyen? She could give it a try without commitment, and it *was* boring teaching youngsters, admittedly. Her mind buzzed with questions but she kept her thoughts to herself and watched the sea. The water was dark, interspersed with white horses. She eyed the sky. It was no longer blue but broken with clouds rolling from the land ahead. She guessed they were well on their way to England, and slowly she was able to pick out a dark smudge on the horizon. England! She had never been there but had heard so much and suddenly itched to spread her wings a little, until commonsense returned. She was an islander born and bred.

'Take the con while I lower the sail!' Danny said suddenly and eyed her lifeline, then clipped on his own. 'Hold her on this heading!'

She hastened to obey, and watched him dexterously lower and fasten his sail so the tiny ketch moved forward more slowly, but still responsive to the orders of the tide on the make.

He came back to her and took the wheel. 'When we arrive you stay here. You will not come onshore no matter what. Understand?'

Louise nodded silent obedience. Then

there was sudden action. Her father dropped the anchor with a thunderous face. Without a word to her he vaulted over the side knee-deep into water at the small lagoon surrounded by tall cliffs. On their port side a large ketch was also anchored. Three men aboard stared fixedly ahead and Louise also stared. Two men faced each other, hands uplifted as if ready to fight, and Louise could see words were being exchanged, obviously hot ones. She watched her father lope over, swing one man around and let drive with his right fist. The other went backwards with force on the sand. The third man stood silently watching, then turned to her father, and with his right hand made some small signal. Her father returned this twice, then took the stranger's arm and nodded before walking him towards where she waited with patient bemusement.

Then suddenly shattering the air there were two loud pistol shots from the top of one of the cliffs. Immediately her father and the stranger broke into a run as fast as they could on wet sand. The beaten fighter scrambled to his feet, looked up at the cliff top, then bolted back to his ketch, where sudden activity showed his crew were hoisting the anchor.

'Aboard!' Danny bellowed. The stranger threw Louise a surprised glance, then moved to the sail. 'Get it up quick! Inside, Louise, and stay there!' he roared at her, taking the con.

'Here they come!' the stranger warned with

26

a roar.

Louise stood on top of the steps that led to the galley, determined to know what was happening. She could just see horsemen riding hard into the cove they had vacated so hurriedly.

'A cutter's coming!' the stranger called to her father.

'Hold tight all!' Danny bellowed as the tiny ketch shot aside with sudden speed and headed for the open sea. It moved so fast it was instantly ahead of the larger, slower ketch. Louise could just manage to see the cutter approaching, also fast. A snap look to her rear showed the beach was deserted except for horsemen, and she could hear pistol shots.

'That was close!' the stranger cried.

'A well put-up job,' her father called back. 'Why did you go to Silas Regnald first?'

'Didn't know you and he seemed expectant!'

He certainly knew, which means there's been a security leak somewhere along the line. Look into this when you've a chance!' 'Not half I will!' the stranger vowed grimly.

'It's not my end!' Danny said harshly. 'Good job we have the hand signal. I'll get you over to France as quickly as possible, then it's up to you. My security is guaranteed!'

Louise eavesdropped in bewilderment. This all seemed like some crazy nightmare or wild fiction.

'He must have pigeons like you then!' the

stranger said. 'That means someone has a loose tongue and the means to get info out!'

'Pigeons,' Louise gasped to herself, which meant Janet was involved—or was she? Perhaps she simply looked after these message carriers and her father saw her regularly. But what was it all about? Keeping her balance, she hastily cut up some more sandwiches, when not reeling against the bulkhead.

'Get below and some grub. My girl will have something ready,' Dan told the other.

'Your girl? But—I thought you had two sons; surely . . .?'

'I do. My firstborn is a bighead I don't trust, and my youngest son is a bit short upstairs, while my girl is rock-solid and bright with it. Best son I bred myself!' Danny explained.

The stranger digested this unusual information, shook his head then stepped down the short flight of steps to the galley. 'Hello, I'm Mike and I'm real peckish,' he announced hopefully.

Louise threw him a swift calculating look, then pushed over fresh sandwiches while dubiously eyeing the little bread and meat left. 'Eat then!' she said bluntly. Were there biscuits left in that far cupboard? She reeled over to explore, leaning in tune with the little ketch's motion.

'My! That was great!' she was complimented by him. Average height, dressed in fairly rough seamen's clothes, which could have allowed

28

him to pass anywhere at a port. Disguise, she wondered thoughtfully, itching to be alone with her father and solve these multiple mysteries—if he deigned to tell her, she added to herself.

'If you're done—here are some sweet biscuits. Send my father down for food!' she told Mike quietly.

Once finished, he was ready to go topside and her father came down. 'I'm hungry!' he began, reading her unasked questions as he threw a slow smile. 'Later!' he promised quietly. He ate in deep thought, then turned to her. 'We're sailing over to France. We'll have a long talk later but I'll need to get my head down,' and he pointed. 'That pulls down to make a bunk. Get yourself some sleep but make sure the cot side is raised or you might end up on the deck, *if* we have to make violent manoeuvres—though I doubt it now. The excise men will be fully occupied for a while,' he grinned roguishly, then became serious again.

Louise saw the sense in sleep but knew it would be impossible. Her mind was in a whirl; too many questions and puzzles and she had an awesome feeling that her life had changed totally, but was this for better or worse? Suddenly she thought of Jack Noyen with a degree of warmth. It was possible life with him would be gentle, kind and open. Yet as soon as her head hit the cushion, which doubled as a pillow, she went out as if pole-axed.

She woke suddenly, with a start, initially confused, then her wits cleared and she sat up suddenly.

'Good!' Danny grunted. 'You've had a sound sleep. Now it's my turn. I've fixed a chair for you topside, but first, here is some money. Go ashore and get fresh rations. If you speak our patois you'll be understood. We're at St Malo, tied up at the far end of their wharf.'

'Our passenger?'

'Long gone,' he told her and yawned. 'We'll not be bothered here, but once you've shopped no one else is to board,' he told her firmly.

'But what if our passenger should come back?' she asked uncertainly.

'He won't. He'll be far away by now. You've slept for eight hours!'

Louise was shocked, gave a tiny shake to her head, hastily straightened the rug she'd dragged over herself and left her father to it, pulling off his boots and eyeing the bunk keenly. Before she'd half-mounted the short flight of galley steps he was lying down thankfully.

On the deck she looked around with interest and wished she could wash, then checked the notes he'd given her. More bread, meat and some cheese, with perhaps a sweet cake or two for afters. Suddenly washing was no longer important.

Later on in the twilight she sat on deck and chewed cheese and broke off a piece of bread from the stick she'd bought. She seemed alone in the world, just a gentle lap of the sea against the little craft and no one else around. Her eyes started to feel heavy, which, she chastised herself, was ridiculous. She'd had a thundering good sleep and it had to be her body clock telling her in this dark it was bedtime. She stood, found a worn blanket, lay it on the deck then curled up under it. She told herself she would only have a gentle doze. So much had happened in the past twenty-four hours it was her confused mind that was to blame—surely?

He woke her again and stood looking down at her, smiling to himself. What a good one she was. Thank all the gods he had her to turn to. 'Oi!' he said inelegantly.

Louise sat abruptly, looked around, then at her father. 'What is the time now?'

'Soon be dawn!'

'I've been sleeping again!' she protested.

He understood better than her. Stress could play weird tricks on anyone and she was only eighteen, out of her depth and environment. He helped himself to the stick and cheese, then squatted down beside her. 'Now we talk,' he started slowly.

Louise was instantly on high alert. She stared back at him, eyebrows arched questioningly.

'I'm still a smuggler but I specialise in

31

people only,' he began carefully, starting to pick his words with precision. 'No need to look askance, girl! If not fully legal it's approved from very high up. As high as one can go. Politics!' he told her.

Louise blinked, her mind shot into top speed and she gave a gasp. 'Spies!'

He grimaced at that. 'You've been reading too many books. I prefer the word "intelligence",' and he paused a few seconds before going on. 'Ever since tribes started to fight their neighbours it has been the oldest, most used ploy in the world, to infiltrate the enemy's camp or town, to find out what's being planned in secret. You know just as well as me how the French have had their eyes on our Channel Islands for a long time, hence the watchtowers built for early warning. It's better to slip someone in the country who can pass as French. Then later get the information back for the high-ups to digest and plan.'

She quickly mulled this over. 'So you're involved in a two-way traffic system, hence all the times you aren't at home!' 'Spot on!' he praised.

'And it's the pigeons Janet keeps with messages or orders to inform you, which is why you call there often? And her late husband was also involved?'

He nodded once more. Then noticed her frown.

'That other man on the beach you socked?'

32

His expression hardened. 'Yes!' he growled. 'There's been a security leak. He's an ordinary smuggler but picked up information on me and decided to try his luck now the excise people have tightened up their activities. He's from Jersey, Silas Regnald, and one day the English excise will grab him. We have a secret handsign known only to the two men involved and changed often just for security. Only a senior government minister knows all details.'

'I take it Mother and David know nothing, Pa?'

'Never, and neither is your husband to know if you marry. Loose talk can cost a man his life. Dead bodies are mute!'

'But does it pay well, Pa?' Louise asked shrewdly.

'Yes, I'll explain,' he began and opened his shirt to extract a small pouch concealed there. Louise stared with amazement. Not many notes could fit into such a small object, she frowned, more bewildered.

She stared as he opened the drawstring on the contents. 'Surely they're not what I think they are?' she guessed with amazement.

He nodded. 'That's right. Diamonds. Never lose their value to start with. Always highly acceptable. Easy to conceal. That's why your pictures have new backings. I've hidden some there. No one would ever guess. You'll only feel a tiny bump, which makes you—you only—the custodian of most of our fortune.'

He spoke in a low voice as she gazed back at him quite mesmerised.

'I trust you always to use your natural nous. You may never have to use them but I can vouch that nothing is more certain than that life is uncertain. When you do eventually have your own place you must find a trusted retainer, an old-fashioned factotum you can turn to if I'm not around. I am very serious?'

'I realise that, Pa, and I'm deeply touched you trust me so!' but she also felt a twinge of alarm. Her father not around? That sounded ominous, especially now she knew the life he led.

'Another thing,' he continued. 'I also have two bank accounts. One for domestic expenses and your mother. The other is savings, and both are dealt with by this advocate. Dealt with this firm for years. Sound as they come, as lawyers. If you ever get a problem you can't manage, go to them. Memorise this name and address,' and he handed her a slip of paper. Swiftly she committed to memory then careful shredded the note while he nodded approvingly.

'And one more titbit of information,' he chuckled, delighted with how she was handling all this. No barrage of pointless questions. Simply a quiet, mature acceptance. 'I've bought a part-share in a quarry, but it's in your name, not mine. If you marry Noyen, good fisherman though he is, a day may well come when extra income could be needed. This too is with the advocate. I think perhaps some time it may be prudent for you to make an appointment to meet him, suss him out for yourself.'

Louise nodded sagely to herself. She knew she needed lots of thinking time now. So much had happened in the last two days. There were so many factors to ponder. She nodded. 'I'll do just that as soon as I can, Pa.'

'And Noyen?' he persisted gently.

She shrugged. 'I just don't know right at this minute,' she explained, pulling a gentle grimace. 'He seems nice,' she admitted, 'but we don't know each other!'

'Go out of your way then. You'll not do better by a long chalk,' he advised.

Again she felt a flash of unease. Why was her pa pushing so? Did he feel so uncertain because of what he did? 'I'll see him.'

she agreed finally. 'Him and his accounts!' Now she managed a wan smile with her thoughts hidden skilfully. 'Now, when do we go home to Guernsey?'

'Right now, and you'll be with Janet for this afternoon,' he said standing, throwing a look at both the sea and sky as well as estimating the wind force once in open water. 'You can take her out again while I raise the sail, then I'll handle her. St Peter Port, here we come!'

It was both a pleasant and long passage to her. The sea was gentle. The sail should have been enjoyable, but too much had happened. She accepted she was another person now, which was both complimentary and frightening. Thank goodness she no longer lived with David and her mother. She was aware that snide remarks from either of them would have made her react, perhaps even violently. There were one or two fleeting seconds when she felt as old as Methuselah with all these new secrets. And there was Jack Noyen!

She stared, willing the town's outline to appear, first as a smudge, then as discernible landmarks, ones she identified. Her heart warmed suddenly. This was her town. Her island. Who really wanted England?

Jack Noyen! She gritted her teeth. She would agree to his request, then take what came next gently. She owned part of a quarry! This was quite astounding. Yes, she must make her number with this advocate. But what would he think of her young years? If he patronised her she knew there would be another reaction and she would likely end up with a display of unladylike behaviour and tongue.

*   *   *

He brought his little craft in skilfully and tied her up after a splash from her anchor. 'Right, girl,' he laughed. 'Let's get you home

36

to Janet's and I'll then put these behind your two pictures. Just you make sure you've remembered all you've been told and

neither wild horses nor storms will make you talk!' he told her sternly. Once again he blessed all the gods he had her as his confidante. It crossed his mind that she'd go and see the lawyer. Once Louise set her heart upon something she could not be turned aside, and he knew she continued to crave the other house. With some females it was gold and clothes, certainly not bricks and mortar. He would never disillusion her but David, knowing she wanted the house, would block her at every turn, and as the firstborn male the preciput law was on his side. It was like royalty, with the firstborn male direct in line. He calculated her odds of getting back the house for herself were far too long for any respectable bet, but he kept this to himself. At the same time, it would be prudent to have a discreet word with the advocate himself and certainly explain his girl's temperament.

He leapt onto the quayside and strode off, Louise at his heels, then alongside him, almost matching him stride for stride.

She threw glances around and frowned a little. It was the same as before, yet all was different. Too much had happened since she last walked here and she gave a tiny shake to her head as her father halted near Janet's front door. She was amused to see him pull a ring of keys from his trouser pocket, select one and calmly open it as of right. He turned to her and read her thoughts.

'Makes life easier all round when I can come and go as I like,' he explained shortly. 'Janet! We're back!'

Janet rushed down the stairs beaming. 'I did wonder when you'd return,' she said and smiled at Louise as she turned to her. 'Jack's been badgering me as to when I'd see you!' and she pointed to a basket one side of the hall. 'He left this for you!'

'What on earth . . .?' Louise said peering at a jumble of untidy papers.

'His accounts,' Janet chuckled.

'You have to be joking! They're just scraps of paper with figures on them and ink blots!' Louise protested. Her father peered, stirred with one finger and laughed.

'He certainly does want someone to put this lot in order!' he commented wryly.

Janet was highly amused at the horror on Louise's face. 'He's more interested in catching fish than his accounts! Anyhow, he left this envelope with money inside for you to buy whatever stationery you need. He also told me to tell you he's bought a house just outside town. A three-up, three-down. He plans to turn one of the downstairs rooms into an office so you'd be able to work comfortably.

38

He's decided it's high time he left his parents to have his own place.'

Louise was startled at this. His own house? Did he have an ulterior motive? Her? She knew she scowled. Her father did not miss this and read her mind. Noyen had been too precipitous and he uttered a silent curse. He'd have to speak to him.

'When does he expect to return, Janet?'

'Depends on the fish. Might be a few days. The weather should hold decent apart from the odd squall. The birds are here, Danny!'

'Good!' he grunted. 'Want to send one out. Will use the desk in Louise's room then get a bird off. I'll make a point of calling in once an evening. Then I'll have to get myself back to the new home and ready for my son's wedding.' He turned to Louise. 'You and Simon must attend, no matter your feelings. Your mother would turn impossible at your absence—no matter how you feel!'

Louise recognised a direct order when she heard one. She gave a nod, which could have meant anything, then led the way up to her room.

Inside her eyes went straight to her lovely pictures, but Danny beat her to it. He lifted them down, turned and scrutinised their backs then passed them over. Her fingers explored delicately. It was just possible to pick up protrusions.

Danny gently unpeeled the backs, extracted

39

his neck purse, removed two more quite large diamonds and jiggled them into position. He pulled a small tube of glue from another pocket, added a dab to each stone, pressed firmly then carefully replaced the backs before re-hanging them.

Louise studied them with awe. No one would ever guess there was wealth behind each seemingly innocuous picture.

'Always remember, if the going should get tough you have the means here,' and he waved at the pictures.

Louise nodded, very sober now, awed at this responsibility. 'They'll always be safe with me and only ever used if the going should get horrendous,' she vowed in a low, almost passionate voice.

'That's why they're here, girl, with you only as custodian!' he replied with equal solemnity. 'Now, a brief message. I must write to confirm the goods arrived and are on their way to wherever. Then one pigeon can go and earn its corn,' he grinned wolfishly.

After he had gone Louise sat in her armchair and slowly went back over all that had happened and she'd experienced since last in this room. Now there was Jack Noyen to cope with! Then her brother's wedding. She grimaced at this and tried to think back down the years. Had she and David always been at loggerheads? Surely it was only when he entered his teens he'd started bullying.

She sighed. She felt sorry for his bride-to-be. A quiet, almost timid girl, likely to become David's doormat.

She felt exhausted and shut her door early, unable to talk even to Simon. Her sleep was troubled as her mind revolved from one situation and experience to another. She awoke with a start, the knocking on her door demanding. She threw on a robe, opened the door and Simon bounded in like a frolicsome puppy.

'Sis! I thought you had to be back. Had fun with Father on his ketch? Where did you sail? What did you see?' he asked enthusiastically.

Louise, wits still a little scattered, collected herself then gave him a delicate, watered-down version lacking all pertinent facts. Simon drank it in but fidgeted, anxious to talk to her.

'And you?' Louise asked him kindly, sensing his need to confide in her.

'I'm happy at the quarry with the horses. I've started off at the bottom but it's fun,' he enthused eagerly. 'The men have been talking about getting some kind of machine in to do the dragging instead of horses. Do you think I could learn to work one?'

Now Louise was taken aback, sharply conscious she was quarry ignorant. 'And are we always going to live here, sis?' Simon blurted out, shooting off at a tangent. 'I like living here with Janet,' he confessed. 'Much better than with Mother.'

41

Louise knew she must pick her words with care because Simon could blurt out tactlessly. 'For the time being.'

'Good! Mother doesn't like me very much,' he confided. 'I'd much rather live with Janet.'

'So you shall, but we have to turn up for David's wedding. Pa expects this,' she warned. 'But don't worry. David will be on his best behaviour to impress his new in-laws. Anyhow, I'll be with you and after a short stay at the reception we come back to Janet's,' she promised, and he beamed his relief at her. Silently she cursed both her brother and mother. Between them they had shattered what little self-confidence Simon had. Did other families have similar problems, she mused? 'Now I've jobs to do and you'd better get yourself off to work.'

He grabbed the open hint and left her to wash and dress, her mind buzzing once more. She felt far more than her eighteen years. Then her jaw set. She would face up to whatever life chose to throw at her. She would indeed be her father's daughter. She would act as *he* would, willy-nilly and with pride.

THREE

George Falla, Advocate, now felt distinctly uneasy. He sat in his favourite office chair and moodily eyed the two shelves of thick law books. 'Damn Penford,' he muttered to himself then grinned wryly. He had been stunned at Penford's words and actions initially, barely able to comment.

'You told all—to a teenage girl?'

Penford had nodded, then hastened to explain. 'She's not like your run-of-the-mill teenagers. I think my Louise was born mature. She's both bright and sharp, she doesn't panic and she speaks her mind. She's tough, through and through. It was time someone else knew the set-up in detail. A bird has gone off though Louise will never sail over there alone. She's not skilled enough. You are that backup with your fancy yacht! Her task will be to hold the fort here if necessary. Look at the days you're in court!'

'Well!' was all he had been able to muster to start with.

'And she'll be coming to see you re her quarry as well as a house she hankers to own. She'll explain in her own good time as well as on other matters, I suspect—once she's sussed you out and decided whether you're to be trusted!'

'Like hell she will!' George had grated.

Penford had then strolled out after delivering his bombshell. Now—she was out there in his waiting room. He cursed once more.

Teenage kids were not in his field, despite what Penford had said. Some friend he could be at times. He tried to peer through the glass but could see only a vague outline. There was nothing he could do. Taking a deep breath he opened the door. 'Would you like to come in, Miss Penford?'

Louise stood eyeing him. She calculated his age as of her father's generation. He was fairly good looking in a rugged way, but his skin was weather-beaten and she guessed that came from the sea. Did he swim or sail? That made an interesting question for later on. He was not as tall as her father but the frame under his suit hinted at power. She sat in the chair indicated while he moved into his to face her.

'What can I do for you?' he started politely, weighing her up. Not a beautiful face but certainly one full of character. That tough jaw line could shatter icebergs. Yes, this one could indeed be a handful, he told himself.

'Pa says I own half a quarry in my name alone. Which and where?' she began calmly, yet wondered why she felt a tiny prickle of unease.

44

'Not exactly accurate. It's forty-nine per cent!'

Louise was stunned. She frowned. 'But that means I can never have a controlling say in its operation. Who is the other partner? Pa just said I had a half share!'

He shrugged. He had a pretty good idea. Penford had not wanted her to have an exact fifty per cent. Did that mean he wanted the other party to work more closely with her for some reason? He must have words with him.

'Who is the other partner?' Louise insisted.

He shook his head firmly. 'All of a client's affairs are confidential. I cannot say!'

Louise scowled at that. She went to take issue, then thought better of it. His face had become a stern mask. Time to change the subject. 'My brother lives in the old family house, firstborn son. To him, it's just a roof over the head. To me it's a wonderful, true Guernsey home. Set in some land, ten vergées, well built with the five windows upstairs. Large rooms, full of character. One day I want that house, but David, my brother, would go out of his way to block me, even if he did have only daughters. We don't get on. We dislike each other,' she explained simply.

He memorised all. Ten vergées, at roughly two English acres to a vergée. Some place, he told himself, for a small island.

'You two always been like that? Foes?'

he asked. Background information was always important.

Louise nodded with a rueful grimace. 'Since we grew up a bit. He's a bigheaded bully. He tried it on with me—just once. I socked him, which he didn't expect. He went flying on his backside so I told him the next time it would be a kick where it would really hurt,' she explained. 'So he bullied Simon instead. My younger brother. He's not very bright mentally and has no self-confidence.'

'Your parents?' he asked quietly, now fascinated with her character.

'Pa is fine—when he's around. Mother is useless. Me and Simon moved out. Pa arranged lodgings. He and Mother have left Cobo, so David has the big house, but one day that house will be mine!' she vowed, jaw set rigid.

This was what Penford had indicated, but he didn't give her much chance with their inheritance laws. Unless some event arose in the future where this older brother would be pleased to unload. 'And?'

'When that day comes I'd want you to act as my advocate,' Louise told him straight.

'Very well,' he agreed, doubting this event would come to fruition. 'And your pa? What does he do nowadays?'

Louise gave him a stern look. 'Ask him yourself,' she riposted. 'He hinted you were old friends!'

So, he told himself. She neither pries nor gossips nor sets out to impress. Penford was correct again. Her maturity was that of one in her mid-twenties. 'Your father hinted you were thinking of matrimony?' he asked delicately.

Louise hesitated. There was no doubt Jack Noyen was a good catch, to use a fishing term. He had been so grateful for her work on his messed-up accounts, and took her strict telling-off manfully. She knew she was getting interested, but in love? What *was* being in love? He would be at home irregularly, not underfoot, which meant she could run their home to suit herself. Simon was quite happy lodging with Janet and she suspected he might never marry. He would never acquire the confidence for supporting a wife and family.

'Thinking of it,' she prevaricated, 'and no! I'm not playing hard to get either!' She gave him a hard look. 'Will you take me as a client if the need should ever arise? I have funds.'

'My pleasure.' He meant it. There would never be anything boring representing her. Indeed, they could even be volatile events. Another chat with Penford was needed.

Louise stood. She was irked the quarry information had not been acquired and she would have a chat with her father. Now Jack would be back and she knew she must put his mind at rest. But—what was—love?

Jack had already sensed her hesitation and after talking with Penford had managed to cool his ardour. Yet he knew she was the one and only for him. He had pondered deeply and waited anxiously for her return. Where she had gone or why he had no idea, and had no intention of asking either. He prowled around his newly acquired house, which pleased him. It needed furnishing, a woman's touch, he told himself. Then he heard her key at his front door.

'Louise!' he cried happily and felt his heart thumping. He strode forward, grabbed her arm, pulled her onto his chest and kissed her. 'And I'm not sorry for doing that either!' he blurted. At least she hadn't backhanded him.

Louise was taken aback, quite unprepared, her mind still with the advocate. For once, quite at a loss for words.

'I love you, Louise. If I don't marry you I'll stay single.

And I mean exactly what I say!' and he studied her expression anxiously.

Louise looked deep into his eyes. They were wide with—fright that she'd rebuff him? It hit her such a devotion was genuine and perhaps even rare. He was nice, she told herself, and whom else did she know like him?

'Don't just stand there all mute!' he begged. 'Say something, even if only to swear at me!'

She laughed. 'Well, where's the engagement

ring?' she challenged, amused how his expression altered from fright to relief to joy. Her pa was right. He was a good solid man. She waggled her left hand, extending it to study a non-existent ring. Eyebrows raised in silent interrogation. 'I like all stones but my favourite colour is red, which means ruby!'

'You'll have the best ruby engagement ring I can discover on Sarnia,' he vowed, and Louise saw moisture in his eyes, which touched her deeply. Never before had anyone shown such genuine feeling for her and, all of a sudden, any lingering doubts were swept into oblivion. She felt her heart go out to him.

'We'll have to take our time to wed,' she warned softly. 'My mother would go mad if she thought we were stealing darling David's thunder. Anyhow, I'm not twenty-one, so you'll have to see Pa. Also I want to feel easy in my mind that Simon is settled and happy. I'll continue to lodge with Janet for a while. You have your house, and I'll see to your paperwork in your office, then go back to Janet's each evening,' she told him quietly but firmly, laying out the ground rules.

He was happy to agree to anything. Also he still had his parents and he wished to expand his fishing. There was good money to be made, and it was work that suited him.

'Simon came down to my fishing boat. He went below and had some good points regarding improving space below decks. Nice kid even if quiet and reserved. I had a carpenter follow his ideas. As to your old man I'll see him as soon as I can. I doubt he'll object to your age,' he stated confidently.

Louise also intended to speak to her father. The forty-nine per cent of the quarry rankled more than a little. Instinct warned her this might give rise to future problems.

'When we can marry, let's have a week in England,' he tempted.

'You've been there then?'

He grimaced. 'Twice when the weather turned nasty. Safer to shelter there than cope with our rocks, especially if at all near to the Black Rock at Casquets. Only a fool gambles in rough seas or a fog just there. Too many ships are wrecked around our coastline. I am very careful indeed,' he assured her, noting a fresh frown of apprehension. 'I never take chances. I have my craft to consider and most of all my crew. They trust me so you must never worry when I'm at sea. When it does get rough I hightail it to the nearest safe harbour.'

'There are four of you all told?'

He nodded. It was wonderful just to be with her and he was anxious she approved of all he did. 'My oldest man, my mate really, is in his early fifties, and I considered I did well to persuade him to fish with me. I was new but had a good smack, compliments of years of saving when a boy and a little family backing. We make a good team and I pay decently but intend to cut the men in on a percentage of the catch. Encourage them even more because it can be cold, wet and miserable work hauling in loaded nets,' he explained, with Louise drinking in each word.

'As soon as this wedding is over you'll have to see Pa and meet my mother,' she groaned.

'Is she really as bad as that?'

Louise snorted. 'She's not had three children. Just one. Dear, darling David. Me and Simon have never counted. One day her chickens will indeed come home to roost and I'll stand there and laugh at her!' she added bitterly.

He was wise enough to comment no further; safer to change what was obviously a dangerous subject to his cherished, his beloved.

A week later Louise grabbed her chance when her father arrived one evening, when she was in her room at Janet's. He studied her pictures and lifted an eyebrow.

'Nothing touched!' she assured him, then extended her left hand. His eyes opened wide as he held it and studied the ring carefully. 'Good!' he grunted. 'Who else knows?'

'Only you right now, but I suppose I'll have to see Mother and take Jack with me,' she said glumly.

'Yes, you will,' he said dryly. 'I'm glad, girl!'

51

and he meant what he'd said. His favourite was settled for life.

*   *   *

'Pa, I'm confused,' Louise started. 'You said you'd arranged for me to own half of a quarry for an income later on in life, if the going became tough. But it's not half. Just forty-nine per cent!'

He was amused and put out. 'Grumbling at a free gift. You should be ashamed of yourself, daughter!' he replied sternly. 'Since when has anyone with half a brain in their head looked a gift horse in the mouth?'

Louise knew she was flushing but she stuck to her guns. 'But why?' she persisted. 'Who is the owner of the fifty-one per cent?'

'I've not the faintest idea!' he growled down at her. 'I told Falla I wanted to safeguard your future and he arranged it all. I just signed the appropriate cheque and two documents, both of which had a name blacked out!' he added. 'I asked no questions either. Neither can you, because you'll learn nothing from Falla. Like all good advocates and lawyers in general everywhere he'll divulge nothing to third parties. It's not a big quarry as they go on this island, but it produces excellent stone, always in demand in England. Guaranteed income, safe as anything in a bank. So stop moaning, girl!'

Louise's jaw jutted. 'But what if this secret partner does something over which I wish to object?'

'Consult your advocate with the objection and leave it to him to negotiate on your behalf!' was his rapid retort.

Louise gave a long inelegant sniff of disparagement. 'Huh!'

'And what do you know about quarries anyhow?' he challenged.

She knew she had been bested but it was not within her character to cede anything quickly. 'Nothing, Pa—yet!'

He turned sideways to hide a spontaneous grin. It was obvious she was going to make an in-depth study of quarries at the first opportunity. 'Are you going to tell Noyen?'

'No, Pa. This is private, between you and me—like your other life and those?' She nodded at the two pictures holding the hidden riches.

'That's my sensible girl!' he praised. 'Now I'm off home. I'll tell your mother you're affianced, then you and Noyen present yourselves for a detailed examination!' he warned, grinning once more as she pulled a moue.

*　　*　　*

Some days later she sat with Jack in the trap pulled by a sturdy pony, with Simon balanced on the rear seat. He was quiet, Louise noted, and guessed it was because they were strangers. She had explained about this young brother and Jack had listened in deep silence.

'He's not like the rest of us in the brains department. His self-confidence is slight. He's had to put up with David's bullying and Mother's snide remarks,' she had explained, 'as well as sneers at school.'

'He was okay with me when he came to my fishing vessel,' Jack had replied thoughtfully. 'I explained the lack of space below decks, he went to see for himself, then chatted on with suggestions. Good ones too!'

Louise smiled. 'He obviously took to you but now he's gone all shy. Our engagement I guess,' she mused, turning and grinning at Simon. 'Now it's up to you to tell us about the quarry where you work,' she encouraged warmly. 'I'm totally ignorant!'

'That makes two of us then!' Jack added.

Simon felt himself start to unbend. He could not remember when anyone had turned to him for anything. He brightened and his whole demeanour changed.

'It's not a big quarry,' he confided, 'but I've heard the men say it yields some of the island's best stone, always in huge demand in England. Carry on, then take the first on the left,' he guided, with rising pride and sudden confidence.

54

His instructions were followed, then with Simon in the lead they reached a strong barrier and below was a gaping void. Simon pointed. 'That's it! The horses are kept quite a distance away so they're not frightened when blasting takes place.'

Louise looked down with awe. What she had expected was not this. An enormous hole in the earth, and distant at the bottom, like tiny children's toys, were men working. They were loading box carts with the blasted rock.

Simon nodded at their tiny images so far below. 'The carts have to be brought to the rock, which can be tricky for horses—that's why the men say machines are going to come. They'll tow something with the rock on and take it to the carts nearby. Then just a case of reloading on the big box carts and off with it to the ships.'

'Moving the rock twice though?' Jack commented thoughtfully. 'That's real man's work!'

Louise could see his argument just as she suddenly saw a wistful look on Simon's face. 'You want to operate one of these steam engines?' she asked gently.

'Oh I do, sis, but I have to get a bit older.'

Louise kept her reservations to herself. It was true Simon had capable hands, but all would depend upon his teacher. It had to be someone with patience and understanding.

55

She continued to stare below. So she had a share in this? Even if not the exact fifty per cent, she would never want for an income. So important to her life, and a secret from her husband. She toyed with the idea of telling him one day, but knew she would not. Her father had dinned security into her being. It still irked that she had no idea who owned the controlling half, but then her commonsense made its presence felt. Did it matter as long as she received the income, with the advocate seeing to that? If someone wished to be silly and secretive, then so be it. She could not envisage a situation where this information would become crucial or critical. If her father could accept this then so must she. The way he lived his life was to be her benchmark for all time.

Jack knew she had gone into one of her brown studies, a place he accepted he could never venture. He did not mind in the least. If she wished to keep her secretive thoughts he was not unhappy with this. He accepted his Louise as she was. Far better her temperament than one with a bitchy or gossipy tongue.

'Come! Let's go home. I'll drop you both at Janet's, then I'd better go and see my parents. Their noses are a bit out of joint at my getting my own home when still single, so the sooner we can wed the better!' he chuckled and gave his fiancée a questioning look.

Louise smiled at him and tucked her arm in his while Simon scrambled back into the trap's rear seat.

'Well, what are we waiting for?' she challenged.

It was later that evening that her father called. 'Hello you!' he greeted her jovially. 'When is the wedding, then?'

Louise was always so pleased to see him and amused as he lifted down her pictures. He studied them, peeled off one of the backs, and inserted a new deposit. She had no idea of the stones' value, but was proud to be custodian.

He re-hung them then faced her, looking serious. 'Your mother has taken it into her head that Simon should come back home as her son!'

'Never!' Louise almost shouted. 'He's finding his feet at last and is happy and relaxed here. Mother would crucify him with that tongue of hers. It's only because David is not underfoot now as a married man. Let Simon continue to lodge with Janet!' she pleaded.

'I intend to,' he told her briskly. 'I'd worked the situation out for myself,' he assured her. 'Just wanted your opinion. He's still underage but I can see to his protection. Your mother!' and he shook his head heavily.

Louise suddenly felt for him. Some married home life he'd had. 'The wedding will be soon,' she told him and sighed. Poor Simon. 'Mother not yet settled even though she's away from Cobo, I take it?' Her thoughts were doing a ricochet.

He shook his head. 'She's a social climber and I thought she'd be happier in town, but not a bit of it. She's flattered at living not far from Victor Hugo, but I've heard he's planning to leave the island, if not this year then next. Done his writing, so your mother wants to flaunt at least one son. I'll deal with her,' he vowed.

Louise hesitated and hunted for the right words. 'Living in town and knowing what a place this island is for gossip, she might have heard about your visits to Janet and put the wrong interpretation on them,' she told him gently.

'She can think what she likes. I'm at home every night when over here,' he stated grimly.

Louise pulled a face. She could well hear her mother's accusing tongue. She could imagine the marital atmosphere. She would not blame him in the least if he had an affair with Janet, who was a delightful person of his own age group. She yearned to tell him but hesitated to voice such words. Instead she lifted both eyebrows enquiringly.

There was a close rapport between father and daughter. 'No, as it happens but . . .' and he let the sentence drop into nothing.

Louise decided it was prudent to move on.

'What happened? Did you find the security leak, Pa?'

Now it was his turn to be startled, and he frowned heavily and, in turn, raised his own eyebrows.

Louise knew she blushed. 'I overheard!' she confessed. 'And what happened to that Jersey crapaud?' she asked using the word for 'toad' Guernsey people applied to Jersey people, just as that island called those in Sarnia 'Guernsey donkeys'.

He had to chuckle. 'There had been a leak—it's now well and truly plugged. Silas Regnald used the best bait to tempt with, money! Now he'll have to go back to ordinary smuggling, but I don't give him long at it. The English customs people have become rather efficient. He'll have to concentrate on what he can get out of France to our bailiwick, or do some honest work instead! And our laws have started to tighten up. Great fortunes have been made smuggling, but those days have really gone. Me? My wares are always human, next door to being legitimate!' and he chuckled. 'That's just why Regnald wanted to cut in. Jealousy!'

'He can't get at you?' she asked delicately.

'No!' he told her firmly. 'There are important people behind me and also I have a backup. That's all you need to know, daughter. Now, I'm off home or your mother will be nagging that I'm away so much—except when I give her the housekeeping. Your quarry share?'

'I'm going to let it accrue and the advocate can invest it for me,' she replied. 'Simon is earning for himself and I'd always hold a watching brief over him,' she promised, and he was satisfied. His girl's word was a bond worth having by anyone. It was also brilliant and rare that she had naturally tight lips. For a few seconds he mused on his three children and how this middle one proved to be the best of the bunch. Breeding could produce strange results.

*　　*　　*

Louise was suddenly in a hurry and Jack encouraged her.

'Let's get wed quickly and quietly!' she said to him one evening before she went to Janet's for the night.

'I'm all in favour of that!' Jack grinned back at her. 'But your mother . . .?'

Louise leaned against him down at the harbour, eyeing the many sailing ships. 'Mother can go and get lost!' she snapped. 'Pa knows fussing is not for me and she's not running my wedding!'

'Great,' he agreed happily. 'And we'll go and see something of England!' he promised. 'Leave it all to me!'

Louise beamed. She felt incredible,

astonishing happiness and knew she had picked the right mate for herself. So Jack organised it all, aided and abetted by her father. They had a quiet, almost simple wedding, which suited them, then went over to England. Three weeks later he brought his wife back. Her father met them with the trap. 'So what do you think of England?'

Louise pulled a face. 'You can have it all,' she replied slowly. 'Too many people, too many horses, carriages and carts around. Far too much noise, hustle and bustle. Too far from the sea. It simply can't compare with darling Sarnia!'

'I second that!' Jack confirmed. 'We're both too island born and bred!' he chuckled.

Danny nodded. They had been and satisfied their curiosity. Now they could settle down as a very good pair. His mind was totally at ease with how it had all turned out for his favourite.

FOUR

1875

Louise let the sea breeze tousle her hair and flush her cheeks pink. She stood by the edge of the town harbour and marvelled at the throng and bustle associated with ships and the sea in general. The quayside was, as always, packed with box carts. There were those full, ready to unload on the ships, and a line of empty ones waiting to be loaded. It seemed impossible for even a rowing boat to hope to find space to tie up, yet she knew it was all highly organised. Even passengers waiting to board stood in an orderly queue.

There were sailing ships, a paddle steamer and a small ordinary steam ship. She guessed it would not be all that long before sail ceded completely to steam. She guessed Jack would follow suit because he was very forward-looking and enterprising. Sail appeared to be doomed except as the wealthy person's pleasure craft.

A smile lit her face as she thought of Jack. He was not just her husband, but her adored pal. Her marriage had turned into something delicious and marvellous, so much did they complement each other. She was astute and sensible enough to admit his working life helped. They were never under each other's feet and the days he was away at sea helped this. Each return voyage to the island became another wonderful adventure of togetherness after a week's separation at the least.

She stood four square and firm against the brisk wind. She wore a dark brown tunic with one of her favourite divided skirts, nearly the same colour. Females of her mother's generation looked askance at such skirts as being far too daring. How the ankles showed and quite a lot else did not suit them either. Louise cared nothing for such outdated opinions, but even she, for all her boldness, did not quite dare to wear trousers. Trust men to have adopted such sensible clothing for themselves, she had often thought!

She looked at the sky. With the wind clouds scudded briskly, which meant no feared mist. The seas around all of the Channel Islands had to be respected, with the vicious layers and shelves of jagged rocks. Like all women whose men worked at sea, the mist was dreaded as much as a violent storm. She was never wholly at ease in her mind when Jack and his crew were out in such treacherous weather.

She stood musing, going back in time. She was now heading towards thirty years, the mother of a lively four-year-old son, and although she'd had two miscarriages she was not concerned. What would be would indeed be. She was almost deliriously happy with life and there were times when this scared her. Her pa had once commented there was nothing more certain in life than it could become *un*certain. She did not see him so much now and she often wondered what his married atmosphere was like. She did know he would vanish now and again for days at a time, and she knew where and for what purpose, though surely the French had given up their idea of taking the Channel Islands? When he did arrive at the Noyen home he'd go straight to her female room, as she called it. It was an extension Jack had had erected at the rear, facing their generous back garden.

This was 'her' room. In it she dealt with Jack's accounts and paperwork and also did her sewing. It was next door to being utilitarian. She had a good desk and chair, cupboards for files and a shelf for favourite books. Facing her was one of her prized and valuable pictures, while the other hung just behind her head. Jack had wanted them in their living room, but she had vetoed this. He had no idea of what was carefully hidden at the pictures' rears, and he had given in to her feelings on this. He could understand the therapeutic value of treasures from her pa, a man he admired.

So there had been no dispute. Indeed, Louise reflected they simply did not exchange words on anything.

She saw David only now and again, if they

simply happened to bump into each other in town. When this did happen they were civil and polite, but there were times when she noticed he seemed on edge. Where had all his bullying bounce gone, and why? Perhaps it was his marriage. Or maybe even jealousy, because so far his progeny consisted of three girls only. In many ways she felt sorry for his wife. She was a timid soul and in Louise's eyes nothing but a human brood mare.

As for her mother, she scowled. Mother had ceased to come visiting once Philip had been born, for which she was heartily thankful. More jealousy from that direction.

Her mind switched to Simon. How he had opened up with those he knew, but he would still clam up with strangers, and girls did not exist for him. Now he was adult they had trained him carefully, aware of his limited mental capacities, but impressed with his skilful hands. He had left the horses behind and drove the steam vehicle with aplomb and skill. He still lodged with Janet but had moved from a single room to her upper floor, which had been made into a compact apartment. Janet provided his meals and attended to his laundry, so Simon was also very content with life.

Her quarry income went into a special savings account, which she had not touched and which her advocate handled for her. Jack was good at his work and provided nicely. It was not that Louise considered they were rich, but financially comfortable they were indeed. And that was not taking into consideration what was hidden behind her pictures. She had never told Jack about her forty-nine per cent share in the quarry, as there was no need. Besides, anything from her pa became strictly private in her code.

She realised she had been standing aimlessly while her mind buzzed back down the years. She had her appointment with George Falla, at his request, and while in town she would call and see Janet, who'd become a cherished friend. Philip would be quite content in a neighbour's small children's playgroup, and Jack was at sea. Quite suddenly, as she turned to go, she became aware she was the focus of attention. She returned the stare and immediately categorised the man as another seaman. He was only a little taller than her but wore a thick seaman's jersey and rough blue trousers tucked into seaman's boots. 'Middle aged,' she thought, 'so what is there about me that requires such rudeness?'

She was taken aback as he left the harbour railing and strode over to her very purposefully.

'You, missus! You're the Penfords' girl, aren't you?' he almost barked.

Louise's hackles rose. 'So?' she snapped. 'I am Madame Noyen to you!'

He gave out a deep-bellied laugh. 'Yes,

like your old man indeed! Rise to an instant challenge,' and he paused. 'Never try and deny it, because you look so much like him!'

This did startle Louise. Did she? 'Do I?' she blurted.

'I'll say. Same penetrating gaze and stubborn jaw line. If you were a man, with his height you'd be his double.'

'I take that as a great compliment, even if you didn't mean to make one,' she retorted evenly and prepared to get on her way.

'No! Don't go—please!' he said, making his tone more friendly. 'Your old man is a fisherman,' he continued. 'I'd like to have a word or two with him.'

'About what?' Louise snapped briskly.

'Just this and that, which could be beneficial to him.'

'Who are you in the first place?' and now her voice became demanding.

'Name is Silas Regnald, from Jersey way.'

Louise's mind raced back down the years as details flashed with clarity. On that never forgotten day when she and her pa had sailed over to England. The meeting between the two men on the beach. Her pa slinging a huge punch and this man going back on his pants. Then the very rapid departure as the excise men suddenly appeared, seemingly from nowhere. And while she was below getting ready to feed a strange passenger, then later the long talk and explanation from her pa.

'You were a smuggler, trying to steal another's cargo arrangement, and came off worse for it!' she challenged.

'I had a feeling you saw it all,' he told her slowly, eyeing her keenly. Of what was she thinking? Her body language had turned hostile. His instinct warned him to tread gently indeed. Like father, so like daughter. 'Perhaps I should have a word with Noyen some time.'

'Smuggling? Not likely!' she rapped back at him.

This aroused his annoyance and he lost his cool. 'You wear the pants then, do you?' he almost spat at her.

Louise lost *her* cool. She let drive with her open right palm and cracked him across his left cheek and stepped forward to depart.

'You . . .!' and he let out an oath, but recovered his wits. 'Sorry!' he blurted and shook his head to clear the ringing in his ears. 'You are your old man with a vengeance!' he admitted, but now his voice was admiring. 'Good job that wasn't a fist. I'd be on my backside again!' He was struggling to joke and placate her.

'Get out of my way, you Jersey crapaud!'

'Okay, Guernsey donkey, but business is business,' he tried once more. 'At least have the courtesy to hear me out!'

'Well, get on with it then!' Louise spat back at him. 'I do happen to have an appointment elsewhere!'

'If Noyen would come in with me we'd both benefit enormously,' he started. 'You see, I've just done two years inside. Lost my ketch and have to start all over again.'

'But that was all years ago when I last saw you!' Louise reminded him quickly.' Furthermore I know my husband wouldn't wish to be a party to smuggling. Besides, he doesn't fish just himself and a boy. There are four of them.'

That was news to him. It altered the division sums considerably. 'Your old man?'

'See him yourself!' Louise shot back and fidgeted. 'I really have to go!'

She brushed past him and strode forward, Regnald watching with admiration and deep annoyance. Louise strode on to her advocate's office. She knew the reason he wished to see her. He was meticulous in presenting her with a statement showing the monies she received for her share of the Benson quarry. He invested these for her at four per cent and as she had never touched these savings they had accrued to a healthy sum. She reminded herself more than once that she was indeed an affluent woman. There were times when guilt hit her at keeping all this from Jack, but she was naturally secretive and her father had inculcated into her that tight-lipped attitude. She must see him now because she felt deep unease at the Jersey man's unexpected approach after so many years.

She saw her father only intermittently, though guessed he would call in at Janet's on a regular basis concerning his birds. He had admired her son. Her mother had not when she arrived unexpectedly at the Noyen house. She had examined Philip when still a baby as if he was an object for sale, sniffed disparagingly and departed silently. Louise guessed it was because David had only girls, and she felt for the daughter-in-law. She knew, only too well, how miserable her mother could make life and the fact she lived in town meant nothing at all. The heir's wife would be under a constant spotlight of criticism. Then she shrugged. David's life was certainly not her problem now.

She reached the advocate's office, entered and smiled at the receptionist who knew her well by now.

'Mr Falla is ready,' she said and opened the door for her.

George Falla beamed at her. She was his favourite client and they were on first-name terms, though did not socialise.

'Nice to see you again, Louise! You look as if you're blooming!' and she certainly did. The picture of health and strength. 'I have the latest Benson's statement.'

Louise sat and studied the figures carefully. He watched her give a little nod now and again.

'Thanks, George. They're fine, as always.'

'Carry on investing for you, Louise?' he

70

asked, though he knew her answer. She had built up a considerable sum over the last few years and, although not rich exactly, she was very comfortable indeed. She had stopped trying to pry from him the name of the other quarry owner, for which he was thankful. One day, he knew, something would happen and all would come out. He also guessed she would have made her own discreet enquiries from annoyance as much as curiosity. She would learn nothing.

'There is another matter,' he began, sitting back in his chair. 'Many years ago Penford asked me to keep my eyes open for someone to work for you, especially to be available when Noyen was away at sea. I think there should be another male available for you to turn to if necessary. I believe your pa spoke of this a long time ago?'

'Goodness me he did, but surely that's history, George?'

He shook his head firmly. 'If you were my girl I'd like to know there was some kind of backup, because—'

'There's nothing more certain than life can be uncertain!' she finished for him, and laughed. 'One of Pa's great sayings!'

'And apposite!' he replied, growing serious. 'Quite by chance I've come across a decent young fellow who desperately wants a permanent job, because ultimately he'll want to marry.'

Louise listened intently. 'Age, education, George?'

'Education very much standard, except in one direction, which shows me up!' and he grinned with an exasperated shake of his head. 'He's one of these people with a natural gift for other tongues. His English is decent. His patois is superb and his French is better than mine.'

Louise sat rigid with focused interest. 'But where did he learn?'

'Simply by listening to other people as he moved around our island. Although his education was very basic there's little wrong with his memory, because his vocabulary is excellent.'

Louise frowned and did a swift sum. 'That makes him about eighteen years then. So what has he been doing since he left school at fourteen?'

The advocate grimaced. 'Just this and that. His family,' he explained, going into detail now, 'are no-hopers. Dirt poor. Live in a glorified hut whose floor is just earth. They live outside town with no sanitation, water or anything remotely civilised, quite content to mess about at anything to get a few quid mainly for drink. Young Sam Mahy is a cut above them, fed up with his family, wishes to sever all links with them and strike out on his own. He's been doing whatever jobs he can here in town, then returning to the outskirts

72

and sleeping rough. I bumped into him by chance one evening. Coming back into town my pony picked up a stone. Sam was the other side of the hedge, unknown to me, getting ready to settle down for the night, when he heard me cuss with annoyance. He came out. Gave me a start, I can tell you! In no time he had the stone out where it was jammed against the shoe. I gave him a pound for his trouble then started a conversation. Talk about floodgates unleashed!'

'And?'

'I was impressed. Decent young chap, just wanting a leg up in life, and I thought of the Noyen household.'

Louise cogitated. 'On this one Jack makes the decision but . . .' She paused. 'I'd like to meet him.'

Falla stood, opened his door and said a few low words to his receptionist. She returned accompanied from a side room by a youth, who stepped in and stood nervously before the advocate.

'This is Sam. Sam, meet Madame Noyen!' he invited.

Louise stared with great interest. She could see his nervousness as he looked back at her carefully. He was wearing a rough Guernsey sweater with rugged trousers and heavy ankle boots. He and his clothing were unclean, which Louise told herself was understandable for anyone living rough.

'You want regular work?' she asked gently.

'Yes, missus. Anything with a regular wage,' he replied hopefully. 'Painting and decorating, gardening, looking after animals. I don't mind what it is at all.'

'Don't fancy going to sea fishing?'

He managed a wan smile. 'Would prefer dry land, ma'am.'

Louise grinned at him. She was taken with him and knew Jack would approve of hiring an outside worker. It was only a short while ago he'd commented they could do with extra help. His life was a busy one even with his wife attending to his accounts and general bookwork.

'My husband will have to see you. He's away fishing now but I expect him back at any time, depending on his catch,' she explained. 'Until then we have a tiny box room. It's unfurnished but I can rustle up a mattress, though it'll have to go on the floor,' she warned him.

Sam took a deep breath and beamed at her. 'More comfy than a hedge, missus.' It seemed incredible to him that a pony jamming a stone in its hoof could appear to solve all his problems. He couldn't help but emit a sigh of pure relief.

'That's settled then,' Louise told him kindly and turned back to Falla.

'I've another call to make first though,' she explained. 'I came in with a lift. Be a good job when they get these horse trams running.

Can you?'

'Of course. Sam, my pony and trap is out the back. Go and harness up, then wait for Madame Noyen to collect you. We'll all go back to Madame's home,' he explained.

Louise turned to him. 'Just want to pop in to see Janet,' she said, 'while I'm in town. Don't anticipate being long,' and she stood for the door. The advocate took the beaming youth with him, well satisfied with what he had been able to sort out. It never entered his head that what he had just arranged was to form a working relationship that would go down the decades to everyone's enormous satisfaction. All because of a loose road stone jammed in a pony's hoof.

'Janet!' Louise beamed. 'It's me, just for a short visit. I don't suppose by any wild chance my pa is here?'

Janet took her in, always delighted to see her. 'As a matter of fact he is. Both of the birds came back this morning from wherever they've been, and your pa is up in the loft. Go on up. You know where!' she invited.

With some relief Louise bounded up the stairs like a youngster again. 'Pa!' she called, and he appeared after shutting the loft's trapdoor, grinning his pleasure to see his favourite. 'Glad I caught you. I may have a problem,' Louise began, then, word for word, she related the conversation she'd had on the quayside.

75

He listened seriously then grunted. 'At it again. Doesn't learn or is desperate. He's been doing some smuggling over here but he'd like to get an England run back again. Would pay better,' he asserted.

Louise shook her head. 'Jack isn't fool enough to touch that with a bargepole,' she told him seriously. 'Why doesn't he get honest work?'

Penford chuckled. 'Wouldn't know what that was! Regnald comes from a long line of smugglers. Both his father and grandfather were in it up to their necks.'

'Can he hurt you at all?' she asked anxiously.

'Not if he wishes to keep breathing healthily!' he assured her with confidence.

Louise eyed him and bit her bottom lip uncertainly.

He read her expression and patted one shoulder. 'Don't you fret about me, girl! I'm a big boy!' he joked and was pleased to see her relax a little. 'What other news? Any?'

Louise told him about Sam Mahy. That pleased him.

'I know Jack will be pleased someone is there when he's away. If Falla made the introduction you can be sure this young man is sound, because Falla is nobody's fool. Also me and Jack were worried about you with those miscarriages. All alone? No! That has to stop!' he told her firmly.

Louise shrugged. 'They were very early ones. I had no trouble birthing Philip, so perhaps the next, if there is one, will be like that. You home for a bit now, Pa?' she asked.

He was pleased with her. She did everything so well. 'For a few days, then away for a couple, then back here again and . . .' He paused. 'It's time I had my favourite meal!'

'Ormer casserole!' she finished for him.

'Right! First full moon and low tide I'll be hunting ormers. I'll warn your mother. Give her her due, no one makes an ormer casserole as well as she does. For someone English born and bred, she took to it once she learned what ormers were!' he chuckled. 'Though it's my job to collect them and get them out of their shells!'

Louise smiled. His passion for this abalone was well known and she liked them herself. Indeed they were considered a true Guernsey delicacy, but first they had to be found at low tide and carefully collected from under the rocks.

'Oh shut up, Pa, about ormers. You're making me drool,' she protested gently, eyes twinkling.

'I'll see if I can find enough for you and Jack!' he told her with his enthusiastic grin.

There was something she had to ask at last. 'What do you do with the birds when you wish to send a message?' she asked curiously.

He considered then decided he could reply

77

when she knew so much already, and had kept confidential.

'There's a tiny cupboard near the loft. Inside are minute strips of paper that go around the bird's leg, fastened with a waterproof. Then just toss the bird into the sky. It'll do the rest, amazing creatures,' he said thoughtfully. 'They always have been, it's their instinct!'

Louise would have liked to stay talking longer, but George Falla and young Sam awaited. 'Must go, Pa!' and she kissed him then departed with a last cheery wave at a smiling Janet.

* * *

Jack finished his steak. 'That was magnificent!' he exclaimed with immense satisfaction. 'By the time we have our catch and I'm homeward bound I can think of nothing but red meat for a change!' he beamed, eying the fruit pie and cream Louise then produced.

'Yes, missus! Your grub is sure good!' Sam praised with equal enthusiasm. He had never eaten such wonderful food, never imagined it even existed. He blessed himself for striking out and away from his useless family. It had been a gamble that had paid off handsomely, and here he sat, a dry roof over his head, tremendously well fed, and all because of a loose stone jammed against a horseshoe, plus his own sharp ears.

Louise knew she was a good cook even if she couldn't compare to her mother with an ormer casserole. It had been wonderful to have her best pal back. Their reunion made up for the separations of his work, but at the back of her mind now was the Jersey man. Did she tell Jack or not? Would relating this to him make life difficult for her pa? Would Regnald even approach Jack? She was uncertain and felt between a rock and a hard place, but then Jack took the matter out of her hands the very next day.

'Guy from Jersey hinted at me doing a smuggler's run. Turned him down flat. I'm not such a fool! Then more hints about your pa,' and he eyed his cherished wife whimsically. 'Told him I knew nothing about your pa's movements or what he did, which finally shut him up.'

Louise stayed silent, just looked him back directly before speaking. 'What Pa may or may not do is Pa's business only,' she said carefully. 'He's never tolerated questions or inquisitions either. He provides for his family and the home and is generous.'

Jack realised this was one of her secrets from him, but was not at all disconcerted. 'I agree with you. It's Penford's business alone.'

Later on he called in Sam. 'You work for madam. She'll tell you what she wants doing until you get in a routine, then you'll know without being told.' Jack eyed his clothing.

79

'I see you're wearing my cast-offs. Bit big for you!' he smiled.

Sam felt embarrassed. 'I only had what I was wearing and I'd been sleeping rough for nearly a week,' he explained hastily.

Jack felt his heart go out to this youth. 'I'll loan you some money and you can pay me back by stages. Get yourself kitted out properly. In the meantime I'll look in the loft. There is some spare furniture there plus a bed frame so you can make your room more comfortable. Got a girl?'

Sam went scarlet and gave a weak grin. 'I do fancy someone, sir, but can't say a word without a proper job and savings,' he explained ruefully.

Jack understood only too well, as he remembered his nervous courting days of Louise. 'Just take it one step at a time, Sam. Now off with you! I want a talk with my wife.'

Louise approved of his tactics. 'Now what about you? Off fishing again?'

Jack nodded. 'Think I'd better. The weather has been too good for too long. It'll break at any time and I'll be under your feet then,' he joked. 'Finances okay?'

'Fine!' Louise confirmed. 'We're not rich, but comfortable!' 'That's the language I like to hear!' he chuckled happily. 'And in that case time I upgraded from sail to steam.'

Louise frowned. 'That means carrying fuel to burn, so surely you'll have less room for your catch?'

'No, that's all taken into account in the construction,' he explained. 'Time away from home will be less and I'll not be so much at the mercy of the weather!'

Louise mulled it over. On such a subject she was way out of her depth. She wondered what her pa would think, then dismissed the question. He was obviously involved in his own affairs and once these were dealt with it would be ormer hunting. Men and their stomachs, she smiled.

FIVE

Louise sat in her little office, letters and work piled on her desk, which she ignored. She felt so low and miserable. It was always the same and never improved despite the many times it happened. It would take days for her to adjust to being alone once more.

It was the same with Jack. He was always so delighted to come home and be with her and their little son, but, after a number of days, he would start to prowl like a restless predator. He wanted his other great love, his mistress, the sea. He itched to be out there once more.

Louise did understand, but it would hurt. She had known his occupation when she married him. Somehow the knowing and the experiencing were poles apart. At least this time she was not alone at home, with Sam still their lodger. The young man was turning into a treasure. His nature was affable and he worked well, no matter the task set. One day he'd get his girl and have his own cottage, but he'd continue to work for them. Long ago her pa had mentioned a general factotum. Someone always with the family, but not of it. She knew Sam would fall into this category in due course, as he matured.

Until then she must carry on and she gave herself a severe shake. It was no good to sit and brood with self-pity. There were letters to write, invoices to check, statements to go out. All had been rather neglected the past forty-eight hours.

She chastised herself. She must stop this wool gathering. Sam had taken Philip to his little playgroup, and now he was back she must get matters organised. With Jack away it was a perfect time to decorate one of their rooms. She sat up ready to call him in when he suddenly appeared.

'When I came back from leaving Philip, missus, there was a man getting ready to knock at the door. He said he wanted to see you urgently, and that he's your brother.'

Louise stiffened. What on earth could Simon want so early in the day? Then the visitor appeared and pushed Sam aside. Louise gasped with incredulous shock.

'David! What on earth . . .!' she began, then her question faltered as he crossed the carpet and slumped in her spare chair. She stared at him, deeply disturbed. This was never her bumptious older brother. His face was drawn, haggard and ghastly white, while his eyes, unnaturally wide, looked at her beseechingly. She felt a wave of ice chase down her spine. Something traumatic must have happened to bring David here in the first place—and looking like he'd seen the devil himself.

Sam stood uncertainly in the doorway. He felt he should take himself off if this was to be a private family matter, yet his instinct was to stay and look after his mistress, especially while her man was away at sea. He felt full of natural protection for one who had been so kind to him, a feeling never before experienced in his young life.

Louise flashed a look at him and read his feelings. 'Stay!' she mouthed silently, without knowing exactly why, except her backbone had gone from ice to jelly with fear. 'David! Speak!' she urged in a low but penetrating voice.

He lifted his head and stared into her eyes. 'It's Pa,' he managed to blurt out. 'He's been found dead!'

Louise accepted afterwards that for a few beats her heart must truly have stopped. She could only stare back at him, speechless.

'The news affected me the same way,' he

told her in a low voice. 'Pa was found floating facedown. The bloke who found him went straight to the house. Couldn't raise anyone. I guess he was too upset to hammer the door, so he just drove out to Cobo to get me. He'd also gone out hunting for ormers. There was a full moon and the tide was as low as it ever gets. No telling how long Pa had been dead, but I guess the post mortem will decide that.'

Louise just sat frozen, unspeaking, her mind in the biggest whirl of her life. 'I can't really take it in,' she managed to get out at last. 'What could have happened?' she croaked as tears flooded down her cheeks.

David wept too, no longer able to control himself. He had dreaded telling his sister. Finally Louise, wiping her eyes, sniffing hard, lifted her head.

'But how? What could have happened?'

'God only knows,' David grated, and pulling out his handkerchief blew and struggled to regain his masculine control.

'No one could teach Pa anything about ormer hunting,' Louise managed to get out, shaking her head with disbelief.

He agreed with her. 'I can only guess he must have lifted a bigger rock than usual, lost his balance, gone over backwards and smashed his skull. A doctor has already looked at him at the undertakers, and he said, with such a wound, death was instantaneous.' He halted again, his voice choking with emotion.

Louise had a ghastly flashing vision and broke into a fresh storm of tears. Sam stood helplessly watching the siblings. Louise suddenly turned to him.

'Sam, go down to the harbour and find someone who can sail out to locate my husband's smack, then bring him back. The crew can stay with the craft. Just say . . .' and she paused, struggling to collect her scattered wits. 'Just say he must come home right away. It's an emergency, but not our son. Don't explain anything else, then come back here. I'll want you to drive me elsewhere once I've been to the undertakers.'

'You're sure, sis?' David asked gently.

'Very sure,' Louise half spoke, half sobbed.

'We'll go together, then I'll have to go home to my wife. I guess this means a coroner's inquest,' and he pulled a face. 'Be all over the island in the blink of an eye. Come on, let's get it over with,' and he stood, holding out his arm to her. A new first in their lives, the siblings walked out closer than ever before, while Sam bolted down the road at top speed.

Louise turned to him just before they reached his pony and trap. 'You are to tell Mother,' she stated firmly. 'We never did get on. Anyhow, my job will be to tell Simon.'

For that he was thankful. His young brother was not his scene and never would be. He realised he was now the official head of the family and Mother herself might be a handful.

Louise had handled this far better than he had dared to hope when he strode in through her open door and sprang it all on her. No hysterics, just genuine shock and grief, but still in control of her wits, and enough to send the young boy to get her husband back. For the first time he experienced genuine respect. His own wife would have gone completely to pieces, he reminded himself, as he positioned her in the left-hand seat of the trap, climbed in, unfastened the reins and clicked at his pony.

Louise stood and looked down at the shrouded form then blanched, one hand at her mouth, as the sheet was removed *and*— there was her beloved pa. The tears flooded both cheeks while her breath came in strained gasps. This was not true, it could not be, it was a hideous nightmare. She looked at David and saw he was likewise affected.

She turned and staggered aside, one hand resting on the wall as she fought for self-control. She took slow, deep breaths and willed the tears to halt. This—for a favourite casserole! Her mind revolved. Half of her tried to accept what appeared to be positive facts, while the other half revolted with disbelief. Since when had hunting ormers been lethal, unless—could Pa have made a mistake and over-balanced going backwards? She felt she must keep any questions to herself. She must go away and think, and think hard. David was not one in whom she realised she could ever confide, even though he was brotherly at present.

She turned to him. 'Take me home, please, then I'll tell Simon. Mother is for you,' she said slowly, wiping her face again. These tears must stop. There were steps she realised she had to take, which were never David's concern.

He eyed her and gave a slow nod. She was correct. First his wife, then their mother. 'Come, we have given the formal identification,' he agreed and led the way with her slightly behind. They had no conversation now, there was nothing to say. Speculation would be idle. It was up to the coroner, and he was glad to drop her off at her home and turn to his personal tasks.

Louise now itched for action and was pleased to see Sam hovering on the watch for her. 'I want you to run me down to see someone and I'll get a lift back. Then collect Philip for me, but first drop a note in for me to George Falla the advocate,' she told him, and hastily wrote a cryptic note. 'Here, see this gets to him. If he's in court or at a meeting leave it with someone reliable. You managed to get a message off for my husband?'

'Yes, missus. Someone was leaving right away and they thought they'd know where the master would be fishing.'

Louise thought for a moment. It would still take time for Jack to get home. 'Right,' she said. 'Run me down to see someone in town, then do my other jobs. They're critically important. I expect by now the event will have spread, but don't discuss anything with anyone, Sam!' she warned.

'I wouldn't dream of doing that, missus!' he replied sincerely. He was desperate to help, to do something.

'Right then. Down into town!' and she hastened to their trap, which Sam had had the foresight to prepare and park outside.

Janet opened the door to her knocking, a beaming smile for her favourite visitor, which vanished as she studied Louise's face. She had been crying!

Louise lifted a hand as she stepped inside. 'Later, Janet. Must use one of Pa's birds, then I'll talk to you. It's urgent. Take me upstairs, will you!'

Janet's face had become serious, but she refrained from questions as she led the way. 'The birds are there, and your pa makes messages with these.' She pointed to some tiny strips of paper. Louise grabbed one and a pen and wrote. She had decided only two words were necessary. *Penford deceased.* Janet held the bird while the message was attached, then Louise stepped outside to a tiny platform and tossed it up. The pigeon flew up, flapped a tiny half-circle then unerringly headed in a specific direction.

Louise turned to her. 'Downstairs,' she said

heavily, and led the way to the sitting room. She sat Janet down on the settee with herself alongside and held one of her hands and faced her.

'It's Pa,' she began. 'He's dead!'

Janet froze and stared back at her with total disbelief as Louise told the whole story, then her own tears flooded once more. Janet was too shocked initially for this. She simply sat as rigid as an ice block, just shaking her head, eyes wide with horror. Louise had to pause to wipe her eyes.

'Did he say anything to you about going out after he'd been here?' she asked.

Janet flogged her wits into action, frowned, shook her head, nodded, and managed to make words.

'Yes, he said he was going home then hunting out ormers as there would be an extremely low tide.'

'I wonder if he walked as usual,' Louise mused, lips compressed.

'I would guess so. He really is—was—a splendid walker,' Janet replied, still shaken by the news. She faced Louise squarely. 'I was not his mistress,' she added a bit sadly, 'but if he'd made an advance I'd not have been backwards in coming forwards, because I thought the world of him, ever since I became a widow. He was a true and considerate friend and to think he has gone—I can't really take it in.'

Louise pulled a face and stood slowly.

'Simon has to be told, but I can't stay,' and she hastily explained about Sam. 'I must be home when Jack gets back. He'll be in a right state wondering what on earth has happened.'

'I'll break it to Simon,' Janet offered, anxious to assist, but, at the same time, feeling helpless. 'Then I can send him to your place, if you like.'

'Yes, I like. Now I'd better get myself off home,' and Louise stood. She wanted to go but also felt the need to stay. It would be better when Simon returned from work. Janet was so reliable and kind. 'There's bound to be someone going my way to give me a lift.'

*   *   *

Louise gave a shiver as if someone had walked over her grave, then she flinched at the sentence and turned to Jack who held her hand. 'I'll be glad when this is over and done with!' she confided as she knocked on her mother's door. She had visited only a few times because of the natural antipathy between them.

'You're here for your dear old pa,' he told her gently, still in considerable shock, having died nearly a thousand deaths on the mad dash back from his fishing ship. Emergency was the word that had frightened him and could only mean something had happened to

90

his cherished Louise. His relief at seeing her, alive and apparently well, had been shattered by her news. Her old man dead? He'd always had a high respect for Danny Penford, and what a way to go—and be found! People had died before ormer hunting but not often, and usually from their own carelessness or misjudgement of the tide. The sea was always a cruel, demanding and relentless mistress.

Louise bit her bottom lip with fresh distress. Down at the back of her mind was the ugly thought of murder. Who was more proven an enemy than Silas Regnald? Yet quick reflection made her stamp this thought away just as the door opened. 'Hello!

You'll be Louise. I'm Betty from next door. I just popped in to see your mother. Your brother will call in after work later on, but he's concerned about your mother. So am I,' the middle-aged woman told her with a weary shake of her head.

'What is it?'

'I don't know. That's the trouble. It's as if nothing has happened. She has passed no comment about your poor pa, as if it's a normal day. It's unnatural. No crying. No demanding explanations. It's . . . .' and there was a pause. 'Go in and see for yourself!'

Louise turned to Jack. 'Follow me in, then when I give you a nod leave me alone with Mother,' she hissed.

Inside the sitting room, Anne Penford sat

comfortably in her personal chair as if on a throne.

'So what do you want?' she grated with a disparaging sniff. Louise immediately weighed up the situation. 'You understand Pa has died?'

'Of course I do. I'm not stupid!'

Louise was initially lost for words and moved aside a little. She placed herself by a window and threw a nod at Jack, who slowly left the room. The sun sent a yellow ray through the window and she had no idea this stance made her a silhouette. Being above average female height, it never entered her head she almost doubled for her father, plus the fact she stood four square, jaw jutting, strength personified exactly like him.

Her mother stared and gave a sudden, violent gasp. Her gaze changed. Her eyes distended and bulged. She lifted a hand and pointed with a quivering finger and arm, which shook violently. Her face was a total mask of horror and terror while she shrank back in her chair.

Louise stood dumbfounded, then understood. Silas Regnald had said she looked like her father in a particular position. The ugly thought dived into her mind again, and with sudden instinct she knew and saw it all.

'You followed Pa,' she accused harshly, 'to have a row with him about Janet. You thought she was his mistress when she was nothing of the sort. Just an old friend of her late husband. Pa ignored your ranting and raving, so when he was bent forward you picked up a nearby loose rock and smashed the back of his skull. YOU killed him!'

Louise was filled with repugnance and her quick mind told her she would never prove anything. Hatred consumed her passionately and she opened her mouth to bellow, then froze. Her mother's body went into some kind of contortion, then rigidity followed while she finally slumped.

'Jack!' Louise bellowed.

He shot into the room, stared then gasped. 'She's had a stroke!' he blurted. 'Saw this once before with an aged aunt. Get a doctor!' and he left the room at a gallop.

Louise stood helpless and immobile while her mind raced. She knew her accusation was correct, just as she also realised this must never be made public because of the important family name. She shuddered to think what the gossips would make of—murder! 'Oh Pa!' she told herself. 'You never deserved this!'

She jumped at the door's tap, then it opened and the neighbour poked her head in a little apprehensively. 'Just saw your husband in a tearing hurry. He shouted your mother's had what he thinks is a stroke!'

Louise beckoned her in and pointed. Her mother sat slumped comatose, breathing heavily with snoring sounds.

'She been like that long?' Betty asked.

Louise shook her head. 'It just sort of happened,' she prevaricated.

'Doesn't look good to me,' Betty murmured. 'There's someone coming!'

Jack appeared, followed by a middle-aged man. 'Doctor!' he mouthed at Louise.

Louise, Jack and Betty stood aside in silence and watched, Louise consumed with complicated thoughts. 'Can you get someone to take a message to brother David?' she murmured to Jack.

He was poised ready for action again. Anything was better than just standing around helplessly. Again he vanished in seconds.

Then arrangements had to be made. 'She must go into a hospital,' the doctor said firmly. Louise nodded. She would agree to anything to end this new nightmare. 'Can you lock up here, Betty? I'll have to go home, a young son,' she explained.

'Leave it all to me. I expect your brother will come back this evening. You get off, Louise?'

Jack drove slowly without speaking. Louise sat mute, but he knew her mind was in similar turmoil to his own. He had no idea of the acute misery and worry consuming her. She was at a crossroads and knew it. So much had been kept from Jack, at her father's wish, so what could she tell him now and, more to the point, should she? Her mind seesawed with indecision. Then she was straight enough to admit she had been ready to accuse the Jersey man of her pa's death. Her instinct had warned her, her pa had never died by accident. She baulked at her mother as the killer, but she knew she was right. It was sheer logic coupled with knowledge of her mother's temperament.

Did she tell anyone? David? That might be quite imprudent. He'd never believe her to start with, and it would mean dragging Janet into the equation. Simon was content living with her, indeed she was almost a mother to him. Janet would tell Simon all that had happened as she knew it, and she'd probably do a far better job than herself, Louise thought unhappily. Too much had happened in too short a period of time.

It would be the same with Jack, much as she adored him. He would be dubious, and going into the depths of an explanation would be tricky without divulging what work Pa had been involved in. She felt it all surge up inside her again and stared to one side, sensing Jack's eyes on her with worry.

'I'm okay,' she lied smoothly. 'Just take me home.' There, hopefully, was some clean sanity, but she knew her life could never be the same again. Her mother—a killer! This was too horrific to contemplate. 'Pa!' she screamed silently as Jack pulled up and halted their trap.

He helped her down, sharply aware she was still on a mental plane he couldn't approach. It was understandable. 'Better get down to the harbour. My vessel could be in any time, if you're sure you're okay to be left?' he asked anxiously.

Louise turned to him and somehow managed a wan smile. 'I'm all right. Off you go. Sam is here with me and I bet David will turn up at any time.'

He frowned. 'Perhaps I'd better stay then?'

'No!' Louise told him firmly. 'I can handle David!'

With a degree of reluctance he did go, anxious to estimate the catch, never truly happy away from his adored sea mistress, but aware of his wife's misery and shock.

He strode off just as David Penford appeared. Sam ushered him and his mistress inside, then hastened away to make a pot of tea and rustle up a plate of biscuits. Anything to help in whatever way he could for someone he too adored.

Louise took David into the sitting room but waited until Sam had poured the tea, who then departed with dignified tact —remarkable in one still young.

'Well?' Louise almost barked.

David eyed her and noticed raised hackles. 'Mother has indeed had a stroke. She'll never wholly recover from paralysis and will never be able to live alone,' he began.

'No!' Louise thundered. 'She is not coming to live here, so don't even think of it!' she warned.

'But . . .!' he started again.

'No ifs, buts or mights!' Louise grated and glowered into his eyes. He hastily dropped his gaze. This was his sister of old, implacable, even frightening, and he knew he was no match for her.

'What do I do then?' he shot back, hitting the ball neatly into her court.

'Simple!' she retorted. 'Sell the house and Pa's ketch, then with the money invested wisely—and you *are* in finance, aren't you!—there will be enough to keep her comfortable in a proper home until . . .' and there she paused. 'But I'll be with you to go through the house. I'll want some of Pa's books, then there is Mother's jewellery, isn't there? We do also have another brother,' she reminded him sternly. 'Simon is entitled to his fair share!'

David nodded. She was correct as usual. If only she'd make a mistake now and again, it would help his deflated ego.

'I think Pa had a will,' he commented, 'so I suppose I'd better ask around.'

'He was close friends with George Falla, the advocate, so you'd better start with him,' she advised.

He made a note in his memo book and suddenly itched to go. Louise could be so overpowering at times, and he could feel hostility for their mother. Did she know something hidden from him and, if so, what on earth could this be? He stood, dithered a

97

minute then turned to depart. 'I'll keep you informed, and let me know when you want to go through Pa's things, you and Simon,' he added hastily.

Louise saw him out. She had been right not to tell him about Pa's murderer. There was something about her brother David she mistrusted, though exactly what this was she had no idea.

Later on that evening she brought Jack up to date with her mother's condition and what had been planned. He was relieved. Having his mother-in-law in his house would never have worked.

'Will you be okay when I sail again?' he asked her anxiously.

Louise had to smile. 'Honestly! You and your mistress.'

'Good then. The last catch wasn't bad but we can do better and the demand for fish is certainly there.'

'I'll be going to see George Falla, the advocate,' she said slowly. 'Pa would have died testate, but with Mother alive and non compos mentis, something may have to be done legally. I don't think David would do anything stupid,' she told him, but pulled a face. Her mother deserved nothing at all, in her code, for what she had done to Pa, but this was a cross she'd have to carry. She often wondered what exactly the advocate knew. He'd left a message in response to hers and arranged an appointment. Why exactly? She felt a sharp instinct prod her mind and, in a way, was glad Jack would be off sailing and fishing soon.

So it was with considerable stress that she went to the appointment, leaving Sam in charge of her home. The best thing that had happened to her and Jack in years was his arrival. He was so reliable and had pleasant ways. He would mature into a fine man for some girl.

She was let into Falla's office, where he stood, grasped her hand and offered a kiss to one cheek, like a Frenchman. Once they were both sitting he turned to her and shook his head sadly.

'I still can't take it in, so I can imagine your shock and deep distress, Louise!'

She felt a sudden surge of tears, lowered her head and cried silently, then looked up at him, eyes still brimming with distress.

'Now tell me all as you found out!' he ordered in a soft voice. 'Penford was my close friend.'

Louise told him most of it, then sat back and waited. He eyed her thoughtfully, knowing her so well after all these years. 'And?'

She took a deep breath. 'Mother killed him!'

He was thunderstruck, fell silent a minute then eyed her sternly. 'Evidence?'

Louise shook her head, jaw rigid, eyes narrow slits of hatred. She explained her logic.

'I hate her,' she snarled, and he realised, at this moment, she was dangerous. He stood and took her hand and squeezed it.

'Go over it all again. Every word, each gesture. Omit nothing!' he encouraged.

Louise struggled and with a valiant effort pushed her rage to one side to concentrate, so that her speech came out as a recital, not a rant.

'It was only when she saw me in outline that she had her stroke, and then, and only then, did I let her know what I had deduced,' she explained carefully.

He listened astutely and analysed each word thoughtfully. Her initial message had pole-axed him, leaving him bemused with disbelief. He considered her words and acknowledged they were horribly accurate. Without her logic he knew he could never have arrived at this conclusion.

'It's true,' he told her, drawing his chair near but still holding her hand gently. 'There are times, when you stand in a certain way, you do indeed resemble Danny very closely. Your mother was unperturbed when told by your brother, and even caustic when you arrived, because she knew what she had done and was not in the slightest bothered. Then you altered your stance, and you must have appeared as Dan reincarnated, which, coupled with some shred of conscience, tipped her into the stroke,' he sighed heavily. 'He didn't deserve to go like this.'

'No, he did not!' Louise almost spat back.

'And there's not a thing you can do legally,' he told her firmly, then switched tactics. 'What did Dan do to earn his comfortable living?'

Louise returned his grave stare with one of her own. 'Why?' she barked.

He had to smile at the sudden hostility towards him. 'Happen I know more than you think.'

'In that case, you tell me!' Louise riposted.

He thought for a few seconds then nodded more to himself than her. 'He was a political courier for England,' and he halted to let her digest those words, then continued. 'And so am I, as the backup.'

Now it was her turn to be astounded, and she could only stare with amazement. 'I'd never have guessed!' she murmured.

'Good! That is how it must be, for obvious reasons. And you've already notified the other side with that pigeon!' he continued, enjoying her bewilderment, which had, at the least, moved her mind to another plane. 'I too keep a couple of pigeons at home, and have a very fast little yacht, though I think the service provided will peter out now the French have accepted the Channel Islands are not for them, and never will be,' he said thoughtfully.

He let her digest all this before he continued. 'Who have you ever told about this? Your husband?'

Louise shook her head strongly. 'No one, and certainly not Jack. I've never told him about my quarry share either, as it came through Pa.'

'Excellent!' he praised. 'There are times when confidentiality must be strict. Keep it that way. Now, as to your mother, Dan had a will, which is lodged in my safe. All had to be divided between his wife and offspring, except you and me are designated trustees for your brother Simon. Because his mental capabilities are limited trustees are to handle his share for him.'

Louise nodded understandingly. 'He doesn't need much money in his life. He has his own comfort zone. Just enough to pay his board and lodgings, and a little for his pocket. He doesn't have a girl. I don't think he ever will because he still gets shy and withdrawn with strangers,' she explained.

He nodded sagaciously. 'He lodges with Janet.'

Louise's eyes elevated. 'You know that, and her?'

'Her late husband was one of us. That's where Dan met her. And after his sudden death Dan took over his role.'

'Well!' was all she could muster.

'Wheels within wheels,' he commented. She had calmed down now with their conversation and had much to think about when she left, which was all to the good. 'You just leave it all to me. Your brother will turn up any time with his copy of the will.'

Louise knew she had steadied but would not allow herself to think of her mother. Perhaps it was providential she had been struck down. From what the doctor had said she might never leave a vegetative state, though could go on for a bit, not living, just existing.

'Pa!' she cried silently. 'It's all been so grossly unfair, and how true your words have proved. There is nothing so certain but that life is uncertain.'

He eyed her carefully. She was almost too quiet now. His thoughts shot back to his friend's initial discussion about her when he had been, frankly, horrified at what the father had told his daughter. How correct Dan had been. She had a backbone of pure steel, was totally reliable and absolutely discreet. Any secret was safe with her and it crossed his mind that perhaps, after all, he should now divulge the name of the person who owned the fifty-one per cent of Benson's quarry shares—then he immediately dismissed such a thought as unworthy of his personal integrity, about which he prided himself, as did any sincere advocate on the island. One day a situation might arise where she'd have to know, and until then that dog could stay sleeping.

'Noyen away at sea again?'

Louise nodded. 'If you mean has he gone chasing after his mistress, the answer is yes!'

and she managed a smile. It was a little wan though.

'And that lad Sam—he coming on all right?'

'He's splendid,' and now she enthused sincerely. 'We'd be lost without him.' She paused fractionally. 'He's proved so reliable and can keep his mouth shut very tight. Unusual in one still so young. We both just hope he continues to wish to work for us and that no one tempts him away with more money.'

'If that is your fear then up his wages,' he shot back at her. 'Always remember, money can talk with a very loud voice indeed!' he advised, and she nodded.

'I'll do that as soon as I get home,' she told him, now standing. 'Jack will agree, I know.'

'You cooled down now?' he asked gently, also standing, and seeing her to the door. 'I don't want to have to come and bail you out of any cell, and your mother *is* going to get her personal punishment. Try to remember that—what goes around always comes around.' He was older and had seen it all before. 'It's wicked the way Dan had to go, but he's gone. Remember all the good times, and all he ever told you. Perhaps also you may wish to consider making your own will as you have a son and might produce another. Look after the pictures your pa gave you!'

She turned at the door. That meant he knew what was at their backs as well. A fortune safely hidden should she ever fall upon terrible financial times. Yes, she should be testate herself, she thought.

'I'll do just that and make another appointment with your receptionist as I go out, George!'

'Take care, Louise. Don't allow yourself to become bitter and twisted. Dan has gone. Just relive the past with him.'

SIX

'Well,' Jack drawled as he finished his breakfast, 'it's time to give you your birthday present. It's a bit special because, after all, it's not every day one reaches thirty years of age!' he teased. 'Sam has had it hidden at his place,' he explained.

'He has?' she asked, bewildered. Sam had married his sweetheart and had his own cottage not too far away. 'But it's only a small place and—'

'And has a good shed at the back. Yes! Here he comes, to time. Look!'

Louise opened their front door and peered intently as Sam wheeled it to her. Her eyes opened wide with astonishment and delight.

'A tricycle!' she cried and clapped her hands with glee.

'You'll be one of the first, but I bet you'll

also set a fashion. Every female is going to want one from now on. You'll have total independence to come and go as you please. No hanging around waiting for the horse-drawn tram when you want to go to town or visit. Philip is at proper school now, and Christine can always go to someone for an hour or two now that you're not breastfeeding anymore.'

'Oh, Jack! What a perfectly splendid present!'

'See, it has good solid tyres and this bracket at the front takes a carbide lamp, if you want to go out in the evening! There is a front brake and even a bell!' Jack pointed, as enthusiastic as his beloved wife. 'Your skirt can't get caught up either!'

Louise stood and gloated, one hand softly touching her new toy. She could not remember when last anything had so thrilled her. She turned, hugged and kissed him then threw him a saucy look. 'You ready to go off to your mistress, I guess?'

He nodded, feeling inordinately pleased with himself. 'Yes, the bass, bream, mackerel and turbot are out there just waiting to be caught!' Then he beamed at Sam. 'Thanks, Sam. Perfect surprise, thanks to you and your young wife!'

Sam grinned his own delight. He was so deliriously happy in his life. A wife. His own cottage, and a good job. A man could not ask for more.

Louise looked up at the sky apprehensively. Clouds scudded along with a very brisk wind. She was island born and bred and knew, only too well, the horrific power of the seas around the islands when a storm blew up, and with all the rocks and hidden reefs.

'What's the wind force, Jack?'

He studied the clouds. 'About force four, might be five in the morning, so don't go fretting. Remember, it's not just my life, but that of my crew, who trust me with their lives. Three or sometimes four of them, depending on who is short of money!' he grinned. 'I'll simply sail away from force four or five and I promise, if it goes up to six I'll head right away for some harbour, either England or France, until it's safe to sail home.' His promise was accompanied by a flashed and meaningful look at Sam standing nearby.

Sam threw him a discreet nod of understanding. Louise would not be alone. She missed this byplay, so Jack quickly dropped the subject.

'At least your mother has finally gone,' he said distracting her as intended. 'I'm surprised she lived as long, if you can call bare existing living—so I suppose you'll have to see brother David once more. Wind all that up.'

Louise nodded. The subject was never of her choice. Her memory was too long and bitter. 'He sent a message to see him tomorrow if in town. I'll go on my trike. That'll shake him!' and she managed a wan smile.

She was still uneasy about the weather, but knew she could say nothing. She'd known Jack's occupation when she married him and even a storm was not as terrifyingly hazardous as sailing these waters in fog.

'You'd better get ready to sail. Can't leave your ladylove waiting!' she managed to quip, and he hugged and kissed her in her understanding.

'And don't you go running someone down on your trike, especially brother David!'

Her brother was astounded into initial silence when she rode up to meet him at St Peter Port harbour. 'What's this then?' he grated and frowned.

Louise felt a flush of temper but bottled it back down and stared. He had changed and not for the better either. Although only a few years older, he looked a good decade her senior. His hair had started to thin and his forehead had heavy frown lines. He was almost haggard and drawn. Where had his stunning good looks gone, and why?

'It's my thirtieth birthday present from Jack. Like it?' and she preened with pride of ownership.

'Huh! That means *they'll* want one too!' he grumbled.

'They?'

'My wife and daughters,' he almost snapped,

then noting her narrowed eyes and knowing her temper he changed his tone, waved to a bench and sat with her, the trike possessively at her side.

'What's wrong, David!' Louise asked gently, unusual for her when with him.

'Everything!' and he swore lustily, which was not in character. 'Shortage of money!' he told her bluntly.

Louise was staggered at first. The statement lacked sense. She frowned and struggled to understand. 'But you earn good money. You always have done. Far higher than what Jack gets, even with a good catch.'

'Not enough for daily expenses, so I'm thinking of taking freelance work in the evenings. There are, it seems, people who always want financial advice or their accounts attending to,' he explained. 'I'd offer a good service at a lower rate.'

'But won't your firm object?'

'My free time is just that and as long as I don't steal their clients it's not their business.'

Louise was shocked by his comments. 'But why are you suddenly so hard up?'

He snorted. 'Because I've a spendthrift wife who has brought the girls up in the same mould. Also that's an expensive house to maintain. She couldn't even give me one son! You have a fine boy in Philip. My name dies out with me!'

'Making a baby is a two way affair!' Louise

shot back at him and managed to refrain from mentioning her younger brother. 'I do believe he's jealous of me with Philip,' she told herself. 'And don't forget,' she said aloud, 'Mother was the youngest of five girls. Precious little dower for her if Pa hadn't taken her off her father's hands. It might be something come down to you from her. Have you thought of that?'

He hadn't, and had the grace, and sense, to go red. He shrugged and pulled a moue. She was besting him again, which irked.

Louise took a deep breath. She couldn't stand much of her brother and his self-pity. Simon was really a much better person. 'There's decent land with the house. What are you doing with it?'

'Why—nothing!' he told her acidly. 'Using the land for cows or anything means a capital investment, then paying staff wages.'

'For goodness' sake!' she said with a heavy shake of her head. 'I think you're being short-sighted, so get on with it! I'm off if all you want to do is moan!' and she stood and grabbed her trike.

He opened his mouth in expostulation, saw her grim jaw then gave a tiny snort. Why had he wanted to see her, he asked himself? She must be well heeled, so had he been crazy to think she'd give him an immediate cash loan? Some financier he was, he berated himself as she swung onto her trike. She gave a tiny shake of the hand then pedalled off. To hell with everyone, he groused to himself in a thoroughly bad mood. He'd do things his way to suit himself and none would be the wiser.

She pedalled slowly, still not a hundred per cent at ease with this mode of transport, aware she was an object of curiosity. She concentrated and improved with every turn of the wheels, until she was confident enough to beam at onlookers. How much easier it would to be wear trousers, she thought. Long skirts down to button ankle boots were clumsy. If only English fashions would change so. She triked on, panting slightly up a slope, and pulled up gratefully at her advocate's office. Right away a tiny crowd of highly interested spectators gathered to study the trike. She beamed at them, suddenly aware she had set a trend. It would not take long before others wanted the same, and why not indeed?

George Falla met her at the door and chuckled. 'New toy?' he teased.

'It's marvellous, George. Just watch me whiz around our island now. Best birthday present anyone could have!'

He grinned with amusement at her reaction, and at the startled, almost envious look on the face of his receptionist. This was going to start a female craze with a vengeance. His wife would be the next, he just knew. He escorted her into his office then settled in his chair and eyed her. She had been his client for over a decade now and they knew each other very well. There was a friendship between them, but also still a distance. He considered he knew her character to the nth degree, and suspected she considered him likewise. He opened a drawer and extracted a legal document of only a few pages and passed it to her.

'There!' he said and almost preened. 'That should shut you up once and for all!'

Louise frowned, took the document and started to skim read at speed. Her eyes opened wide with shock, she gasped and looked over at him with some bewilderment. 'But . . .!' she began, and paused to read over clauses again, at which she shook her head and pulled a face. 'What exactly has happened—after all these years?'

'My first reaction was the same, then I obtained facts. It's true! You now have your fifty per cent of Benson's quarry at last. Pleased?'

'Delighted, but also bewildered!' and she halted with a frown. 'So do I now learn the other owner?'

'Yes! It's been me for the last two weeks!'

She shook her head once more. 'Start at the beginning, George!' she begged.

He settled back more comfortably in his chair. 'Quite simple. The previous owner put himself in a real financial mess through gambling and had to have money and in a hurry. He bought originally as a financial investment then started betting in England

112

and wasn't very good at it. He offered it all to me so I bought him out, lock, stock and barrel, and he's hightailed it back to England, and don't ask his name either. I'll have my share as a cushion for my old age, and when I've had enough of the law in general. Thought you'd like that odd one per cent, which has always stuck in your throat, hasn't it?' he teased. He watched the expressions chase over her face.

'You've been very fair and straight with me, George,' she said gently. 'Thank you! Yes, it has always riled me and you needn't have told me at all,' she praised.

'Right. Let's call a halt to the mutual admiration society and get down to business. I don't like the way Benson's has been run. As quarries go it's a small one compared to others here and on Jersey, but it yields good stone. It's been mismanaged though, and I suspect for years. The old story of the absent boss. Take the crane for example. Just one. Ridiculous! There should be at least two, and on rails to move them around easily. More stone can be shifted with pairs working in unison.'

He paused to collect his thoughts then continued. 'I've gone into this matter in depth. As I say, two cranes on rails working in tandem can easily shift the blasted rock into the Tippa trucks towed by the small steam puller. It's taken to where the rock is dressed to the buyer's specification. Goes back in the Tippa truck and is then placed in the box cart. It's taken to the harbour and shifted onto the ship with their harbour crane. The aggregate can simply be put in other box carts with a shovel at the crane's end. At the harbour this is simply poured into the ship's holds. Noisy and dirty but efficient,' he explained, with Louise listening enthralled.

'Then?'

'Some of the larger quarries have these steam pullers and Tippa trucks on rails too but Benson's is too small.'

'We don't cover enough ground?' Louise asked.

'Correct!' he confirmed. 'We'd have to be a fair lot bigger to make such a viable enterprise so we'll have to see the current manager some time and go into matters with him.'

'I follow you on this, George, because I know so little. I must learn more!' Louise vowed.

He grinned back at her. 'I've had to do that myself by asking around, questioning and listening,' he confided.

Louise grimaced a little. 'I feel positively ignorant,' she confessed, 'so you'll have to make sure you pass your learning on to me!'

'When the time is appropriate we'll call the manager in. He knows about me as a half owner. I think he's bursting with curiosity to learn who the other is!' he chuckled.

She realised she was ignorant to start with, but now she had the incentive to absorb knowledge. 'Go on, George!' she encouraged.

'Some chunks of blasted rock can weigh up to seven tonnes, and they have to be moved to where this rock can be dressed by the banker masons, as they're called. The rock must be in manageable precise portions, often to a specific size and shape. Don't forget, it's our best financial export, especially to England. Men who work these cranes are very highly valued. Mature and with considerable experience. They must be capable of estimating the weight of the rock against the strength and capability of their crane, otherwise the crane is pulled over and there is a horrendous death.'

'My younger brother works at Benson's. Pa arranged this for him long ago. He drives some little steam engine that pulls trucks until the horses can take over to go to the harbour,' she said thoughtfully.

He nodded. He already knew that. 'That's simple steam engine driving,' he assured her. 'Just stop, start, go, left and right. Don't forget, men who work in quarries are a special breed, like coalminers and fishermen. You can pick them out going to work. They wear iron-shod clogs to protect their feet and always carry their cans with tea and food packets. They work out of doors in all foul weathers, just with their tools, hammers, sledgehammers, crowbars, and there is always a blacksmith engaged because their tools blunt easily.

The cranes need specialist men. It's also dangerous work in another way. Too much fine dust, especially from the silica in the rock, which is there naturally. Too many years at this work and men can get silicosis, a lung disease, which can be very fatal indeed. Yet the previous owner was short-sighted. Only one crane instead of two at least, and some of the little steam engines for pulling, as your brother would use, were hired. Stupid. I think we should go into all this very thoroughly, modernise. Cut out all rentals, buy instead, but it will take some time to sort it all out,' he warned her.

'There will also be the books to attend to,' Louise said thoughtfully. 'I attend to Jack's fishing accounts, pay his men, work out their bonus on the agreed partnership basis, and so on, which is why he never has trouble getting crew if someone falls ill.'

'Sensible! But I can't see you'd have time for the quarry books. I certainly don't with my legal work,' he mused thoughtfully.

'I'd like to try. I have Jack's affairs so nicely organised I'm sure I could manage after a few weeks. How about it, partner?'

He considered then nodded slowly. 'Give it a try and see how it works out,' he suggested, which delighted her and he paused thinking deeply. 'We could do with a copy each of the bills, statements and invoices.'

'Simple, I'll copy them out. Jack told me

a while ago the Americans have some kind of invention that saves handwriting. Some machine that produces print when keys are pressed. When they become available he's going to get me one, but until then it's all by hand as usual,' she told him.

He nodded. 'I've also heard about it. I think it's called a typewriting machine. There is another point I'll raise now, as good a time as any.'

Louise stilled. His face wore its solemn look. 'Go on, George.'

'I must compliment you. Dan was right. You do indeed have close lips and lack of questions, so I'll tell you now I no longer keep pigeons. That's all over and done with. Plenty of steamer services between England and us here, as well as France. So simple to get around now. And there is one final point. Apart from my legal affairs there are no secrets between me and my wife. Have you told Jack about the quarry yet?'

Louise shook her head. She considered a few moments then threw a wan smile at him. 'I think I will now when he's next at home.'

'Soon?'

'Depends on the weather and the fish.' She dimpled.

'Good!' he praised. 'If you can't trust him after all these years it has to be a rotten marriage!' he chided. 'He doesn't need to know anything about what Dan did,' he had to warn.

'He won't!' she promised solemnly.

'Then in that case off you go and startle more people with your new gadget. I have some work to do before I'm in court!'

Louise felt both thoughtful and guilty as she went home. So much had been kept from Jack, mostly from necessity—her pa's past life, as well as the hidden diamonds. She decided she would relate only the quarry even now, and looked up at the sky. The clouds were higher and not moving so fast. The wind strength had dropped. If the fishing had been good Jack could be home at any time. Steak! She must get in the very best for him. After days of eating fish, eggs and bread he would hanker after and crave red meat, grilled slowly, with gravy, and all the trimmings. Only after he had eaten would she talk.

A week later she had her chance as they sat in their living room, Jack beaming happily with a full stomach.

'Feel better now?' Louise teased him gently while she sorted out her words carefully. 'Want to have a chat with you now everyone's fed and in bed,' she started delicately. 'Been keeping a secret from you and it's time I told.'

Jack threw back his head and let out a bellow of amusement. 'You've kept secrets from me since before we were engaged!'

Louise was startled. 'But . . .?' she began, then floundered to a halt.

'You and your pa were a good pair!' Jack told her, still grinning at her sudden confusion. 'Especially your pa, with his people smuggling!'

Louise was shocked into silence. She took a deep breath, determined to try again. 'What exactly do you mean?' she asked warily.

Jack shook his head. 'I know most of it. That Jersey man Silas Regnald has a mouth and he told me your old man socked him one and it's always rankled because his crew saw it all. Then he was caught and went to prison and when he came out he sounded you out about me doing some runs for him. When I refused he threw the rest at me. Not a very nice piece of work, and with a long, resentful memory to boot. He worked it all out, like me. Your pa's death finally shut him up on that road. He also knew Janet was involved and had seen pigeons taking off from the roof.'

'Janet was never, never involved. Pa was just a close friend of her late husband. Nothing more, nothing less!' she said hotly. 'That odious man wants to spend more time on Jersey and stop coming over here!'

'I've always realised you had secrets from me, but I'm not a nosy bloke,' he said sincerely. 'I guessed all along you had your reasons and you were close to your pa while he lived. So be it. Amen!'

'Oh Jack!' she said softly and held his hand. 'Pa swore me into secrecy and I could not let him down, but what I'm going to tell you now is because it came from him,' and she took a deep breath. 'I own half of Benson's quarry.'

'You what?' he gasped, his turn to stiffen with complete shock. 'Say again!'

'It's true! Pa bought me in when I was only in my teens, at the time you were courting me. He wanted me to be completely independent financially at all times no matter what life threw at me. For years I had just forty-nine per cent, but now it's fifty,' and she explained what she'd been told recently by her advocate.

He listened in stunned silence. 'But where is the money from your share?'

'Invested in English pounds by George Falla over there. I've never touched any of it.'

'Good God! You must be worth something by now!' he exclaimed with amazement.

'And,' Louise told herself, 'that's without Pa's diamonds too!' 'Am I allowed to ask how much?'

'About 450 English pounds?'

'Good grief!' he exclaimed, then a new thought struck him. 'You're saving it for something,' and he crinkled his forehead while he worked it all out. 'I know!' he gasped. 'It's for that house you've always wanted. Your parents' old house at Cobo, which belongs, in law, to your brother David!'

Louise nodded and pulled a moue. 'He knew I always did want it, so on the odd occasion I meet him I'm careful to say nothing.

He would be odious with his crowing!'

Jack considered this. 'Strangely enough I bumped into him the last time I was ashore. Nearly didn't recognise him. He's only a couple of years older than you but looks more like ten.'

'Money problems,' Louise explained. 'It came out a bit the last time I spoke to him. I suspect he was going to try and get some kind of cash loan from me, but I acted dumb.'

Jack gave a snort. 'What made him marry into that rich family? Thought he'd be onto a good thing? Not with them. An in-law is not close family to them, and they're rolling in money. They made it from organised smuggling when there were fortunes in running spirits, like rum and brandy over to England, as well as anything else the English wanted. And great fortunes they were, until the excise laws tightened up both in England and here. They just invested their monies and sat back to enjoy their lives. First the grandparents, then the parents, finally the last generation. The smuggling has long gone. The profits have not. Your brother would have found out, set his cap at their oldest girl and the rest you know, but it's not turned out as he hoped. He'll always be the outsider to them and, at the same time, the daughter he married has always been used to having everything she wants as and when!'

Louise shook her head. 'I didn't know about

any of this.'

'I bet your pa did!' he said thoughtfully. 'Precious little was missed by him.'

'I don't want him or anyone to know about Benson's until it becomes necessary. My partner is the same. You now know and probably I'll tell Sam in case I have to be driven there some day when you're at sea. Sam is remarkable for keeping his mouth shut tightly. We are so lucky to have him.'

'That's another point. Sam and his missus live in a rented cottage, which is not the best. I suspect he'd like to buy a little property for them both. How about upping his wages and helping him to get some kind of mortgage, and standing as his guarantor?'

'What a splendid idea. Why didn't I think of it!' she scolded herself. 'Speak to him about it before you go rushing off to your mistress again!'

'Will do later on today. And how is that lovely little girl of ours? I swear I've never seen such a beautiful child before!'

Louise grunted and pulled a face. 'Handsome is as handsome does!' she said a bit tartly. 'I hope she's not going to give me boy troubles in her teen years. Remember, girls bring them home! And she's a mind of her own. Inclined to be argumentative!'

Jack bellowed with genuine mirth. 'In that case she just takes after her ma! You've never been acquiescent, now have you!' he jested and she threw him a mock punch.

He became serious then. 'I hope you don't still fret when I'm at sea?'

She was truthful. 'Can't help it. The sea is so powerful and we are so puny in comparison. I get truly scared though when the mist comes down but,' and she gave a tiny shrug, 'it's your living and life.'

'Bless you, dear wife. Hark! That sounds like Sam. Sam!' he bellowed. 'Come in, please. We want a brief chat with you before you go home.'

Sam entered, conscious he was in gardening trousers and boots in a room of fine furniture and carpets. He stood just inside the open door, uncertain and embarrassed. Had he done something wrong? What could this be?

'Come right in, Sam,' Louise said understandingly. 'The carpets can soon be brushed again.

'What are your thoughts on buying your own place? We'd be in a position to stand as mortgage guarantors,' Jack said.

Sam blinked, his eyes opened wide and he beamed. 'That would be marvellous, sir, but I don't have enough for even a little deposit,' he told them ruefully.

'While I'm next away my wife will see to that, and if your better half wants a job and can cook, there's one for her here,' Jack added, flashing a meaningful look at Louise, who nodded keenly—if the girl could cook!

'Does your Sal cook well?' she asked gently.

Sam laughed with delight. 'That's why I married her, missus. A man has to look after his stomach!'

'Then that's settled. Go and see the advocate Falla when you find something suitable. He won't handle it himself. He's far too involved with work in the States—our courts. He'll supervise a conveyancing junior. Okay, Sam?'

Sam felt like turning cartwheels. This was somewhere his wildest dreams had never dared to take him, as well as his beloved Sal. 'I can hardly take in what you're both saying. I'm so grateful. More than you good people will ever know,' he told them sincerely and felt a ridiculous lump lodge in this throat. All this had come about because a pony had jammed a stone in a horseshoe. Thank God he had walked away from his rowing, drinking, horrible family with their miserable, unchanging existence.

Jack slapped his shoulder. 'And now there is something you can do for me,' he began.

'Anything, sir!' Sam vowed.

'Whenever I'm away at sea and shall I say something unusual happens, I ask you to escort my wife to wherever she wants to go. Use your total discretion with my full authority. You acted so splendidly when Penford died so unexpectedly, even if I did die a thousand deaths on the fastest sail back to this island I've ever made. And you, wife, will not stand in his way at all. That's a marital order!'

Louise prepared to argue, then studied his stern facial expression. It was one she rarely saw, and she had a flash of empathy regarding his feelings for her once he had sailed. She smiled, deeply touched but could not for the life of her think of any situation that might require another emergency message sent to him.

It was only weeks afterwards that they both wondered, with awe, whether Jack had been struck with a thunderbolt of prescience.

Her mind switched to more mundane and practical activities. 'If Sal could start in the morning you can sail off with a better diet. How about a roasted whole leg of ham with chutney? That would be a change from eggs, cheese—and fish. More home-baked bread and biscuits. How many of you altogether, Jack?'

He was very interested. 'Four, including me!'

'In that case it will be two whole legs of ham!'

'My Sal will be here first thing in the morning, missus, with me!' Sam vowed. He would never hesitate to run his blood to water for this couple. He wished they were his blood relatives but they were not, so this had to be the next best thing.

SEVEN

Louise had just sat with work on her desk when her door opened with a violent bang, which made her jump with shock.

'Sam!' she protested, staring. He slumped in the nearest chair without being invited, chest heaving, face red, eyes wide and shocked. 'Oh, missus!' he cried. 'It's Benson's quarry, where your younger brother works. There's been an explosion and he's been killed!' he blurted.

Louise felt ice slither down her spine as had happened years ago with the news of her beloved pa. She swallowed heavily and looked helplessly over at Sam who struggled to regain personal control. She shook her head and fought internally. 'How?'

'It was the boiler of that little steam puller, as I call them, it suddenly blew up with no warning!' and Sam stood. 'Whenever master's away I keep the pony in the stable, just turn her out at nights. I can be harnessed up in no time to drive you there. It's my duty, missus!'

Louise was too shocked and aghast to say anything constructive. She gave a feeble nod and tried to control her spinning wits. How could this happen a second time in her life?

Afterwards she could remember few details. Sam appeared within a few minutes, it seemed, and she was being taken to the quarry. Simon dead? It did not make sense. Gentle, happy Simon, content in his own little world.

There was pandemonium at Benson's. Men milled around. Officials bustled everywhere as Sam helped her alight and gave her his arm, for which she was suddenly glad. She walked forward uncertainly. To one side was mangled metal, still steaming, and something covered with a hastily thrown blanket. Men eyed her, gathering in small groups, talking among themselves, but this ceased at her approach.

'Madame Noyen. The deceased is her brother!' Sam told them, and an official, removing a battered helmet, strode forward.

'Madam. I'm Smythe. The site manager. I don't know what to say to you,' he started nervously. An hysterical female was the last person he wanted around, but if she was kin she had the right to know. 'It all happened so suddenly. Your brother never suffered. He knew nothing. One wouldn't with a steam explosion,' he started, trying to be tactful and failing completely.

'How often does this kind of thing happen?' Louise asked in a controlled voice, though she trembled inside.

'Never happened before, and I've been here years, madam,' and he paused. 'Don't see him, please. Remember him as he was.' Thank the gods she was under control. He simply could not manage a sobbing, screeching female. He flashed a look at her young male escort. Where he fitted into this equation he neither knew nor cared. All hell was going to be let loose with the owners, and he had been informed they were new. He had yet to meet them or know anything about them.

'Surely these pullers are serviced regularly?' Louise asked quietly, fully under control now.

Sam nodded and chimed in. 'They have to be,' he said firmly, 'else pipes can fur up, weaken the boiler against hot steam and—' He waved a hand.

The manager knew the young man was correct. Who was he?

'This quarry has had new owners for the past few weeks. The old owner saw to all servicing of equipment, except the crane, which my own senior men did,' Smythe explained hastily.

'I will want full details. I own a half share of this quarry,' Louise said quietly.

Everyone stared at her with amazement, especially Sam. Smythe was speechless, and the workers just talked quietly among themselves and stared at her. A woman quarry owner? Had the world gone mad?

Smythe was lost for words, so Louise decided to help him. 'Myself and my partner will shortly convene a meeting with you—there is much to discuss. You will hear from him within a few days.'

He struggled for words. 'Very well, madam,' he managed to get out and nodded at Simon's body. 'Shall I . . .?' he asked nervously. 'I think your partner's called Falla?' he pried.

Louise gave him a brisk nod. 'Yes, George Falla, the advocate for the States.' Tears were not far away and she flashed a look at Sam, who understood immediately and placed her hand on his arm and half turned for the trap. He had a task to do and the sooner the better.

He would tell her on the ride back. This the master had to know, and then there would be the lady where Simon lodged. A funeral. An inquest. The mistress must not be left alone in the house until the master could return, and that would take time. He would move back into the spare room, so, at least, she was not alone at night, always the worst time. When his Sal knew she would certainly agree.

Sam eyed her as he drove gently. 'I'm staying with you until the master gets back, missus. Sal will agree with me too. I'll write a quick note to him then get off to the harbour.'

Louise felt a wave of gratitude fill her, which somehow managed to abate more tears. She realised she was in shock. 'I appreciate that, Sam, but tell my husband not to rush back. Nothing can be done—yet,' she added thoughtfully. She must have a deep, serious talk with her partner. Had Simon's puller been serviced and, if not, why not? Another point struck her. 'Sam! When you get back from the harbour make sure whoever sails out will be well paid. Go and tell Janet. Bring her to my home, if she wants to come too. She'll be in shock as well. She treated Simon like a son. I don't suppose you know any young fellow who wants good lodgings?'

Sam turned to her and just walked the trap slowly. 'As a matter of fact I do, missus. My mate Ben. We go out and have a couple of pints twice a week. He's not married and does not have a steady girl. Says he's playing the field, but he works in town and still lives with his parents way over at Pleinmont, Torteval.'

'That is a distance to journey twice a day,' Louise agreed.

'He's said more than once life would be easier living in town and just go home for Sundays,' Sam added.

'Arrange it, Sam, if you think fit. At the same time make an appointment for me to see my advocate as quickly as possible,' and her face became grim. 'There's things to investigate without too much delay. Then brother David will have to be dealt with,' and now she scowled. More tears could appear later on in bed, she vowed. She owed it to Simon to ask questions and get answers. George Falla would be the same, she knew.

Sam took a deep breath then simply had to come out with it. 'You really own half of Benson's, missus?'

'Yes, Sam, I do, and thereby hangs quite a story. In due course I'll satisfy your curiosity.'

'Sorry, missus. Didn't mean to pry. Was

130

just so shocked when you came out with it. So was every other man there!' and he smiled, visualising again the stunned looks on everyone's face. He pulled up and took her inside her home then shot away to put Sal in the picture. Upon his return Louise gave him writing materials for a short note to be taken to Jack, wherever he was. She offered some Guernsey money. She didn't have any English money, which was of a higher value, and Sam carefully selected two pounds.

'Will that be enough?' she asked anxiously.

'More than enough, missus,' he replied flatly.

Louise felt tears hovering, 'If Janet comes back with you and my elder brother turns up, arrange it so we can talk privately, in my office, I think.'

Then Sal appeared with a pot of very hot tea and some brandy. 'I don't know what to say to you, missus, so get this down you with a slug of brandy.'

Sam departed in a flurry of activity and Louise drank slowly as the whole awful day now hit her with force. Tears flowed and Sal, so young herself, sat silently and helpless. How long they sat neither knew, when the door banged open and Sam was back, with David in tow. 'Missus, go in your office with your brother Janet is outside. She'll sit with us for the time being.'

With the door shut firmly Louise settled in

131

her chair and poured a second cup of tea with a slug of brandy. 'Drink, David!' she ordered quietly.

'I can hardly take it in,' he murmured shaking his head at her. 'What the hell happened?'

'It will come out at the inquest, but I guess his steam puller wasn't serviced. That may have been Simon's fault not understanding,' she admitted heavily.

'Never heard the like before. I do know they use them a lot at the slate quarries in Wales. Never heard of one exploding either. The owners will have to look into this very thoroughly, though I gather one of them has left the island, sold up and gone to England. Don't know who the other partner is.'

Louise gave him a steady look and sprang her bombshell. 'It's me!'

He looked at her quite speechless, eyes wide with shock. 'But how—when?'

'I didn't have a full half share until very recently, so was never involved. Pa bought me in long before I married Jack. Because I was a girl he was anxious I should have financial independence at all times, and he didn't like people knowing his business movements and affairs.'

'I can't take this in either!' he gasped, shaking his head again with shock and bewilderment. 'You own—half of Benson's?'

Louise just nodded, slightly amused at his

expression. She had a shrewd idea what might come out shortly if he was so hard up, and she wondered how he would take a negative response. He looked drawn and haggard. Where had the handsome young man gone? She remembered what she'd been told about his in-laws. It certainly appeared to be the case of marrying in haste and very much repenting in leisure. She wondered what Pa had thought about it all. She still did not like this brother and neither did she trust him, though she was honest enough to admit he had done nothing negative to her and Jack.

'If you own half of Benson's plus what Noyen earns fishing you must be very well heeled indeed. Much more so than me, so here goes,' he said taking a deep breath. 'Do you want to buy my house, sis?'

Now it was Louise's turn to be struck dumb. She could only stare at him while her mind spun, with none of it making sense. 'The house?' she parroted a little helplessly. 'Now I don't understand,' she said, her voice riddled with confusion, her brows drawn in a heavy, perplexed frown.

He gave a snort. 'Dead simple. I'm not staying on this island. Much too stultifying now for me, and also I intend to get away from the in-laws once and for all. Put some distance, some sea between my family and them. They're all too fond of running up there for money, as it appears I don't provide enough.'

'Don't you love them anymore, David?'

'Love? Love! What's that to do with it all!' he said bitterly. 'It turned into a mismatch marriage. There was someone else but she came from a poor family, so I dropped her!'

'Oh David!' and for the very first time she felt genuine empathy for him, especially when she thought of her own wonderful, happy marriage. She struggled with tangled thoughts. This was the brother for whom she'd had years of detestation. Now?

She answered her question honestly. Perhaps part of the problem had been of her own making? Had she been too quick to condemn and fight him? When had she made a positive effort to be a sibling friend? But perhaps her mother had been bent on ensuring that didn't happen? Now he was drawn, haggard and had turned to her. And the house! She acknowledged this was his bait but at least he had come to her whatever his true motives were. Quite suddenly, to her shock, she found warmth for him. They were the only two left of the Penford family now.

'Oh David!' she said and turned four square to him. 'I've always adored that house but don't ask me why,' she added hastily and pulled a face. 'Because I do not know and no! I'm not mad either!'

He threw her a wide grin. 'No?' he drawled, then laughed at her expression. 'You could have fooled me, sis!' and he paused. 'I made a mistake and I've paid for it, so we're all going to live in England, but you're the only one who knows yet, except Aunty Joan.'

'Pa's young sister in Bristol!' she gasped.

'Exactly. I've been in touch with her by letter, sworn to secrecy of course, so I thought of you and the house. You were always crazy about it and the Cobo region. What about it?'

Louise gasped and shook her head. 'You've sprung it on me!' she protested. 'And Jack is away at sea, and we do have a nice house and garden here.'

'You can have it for 500 English pounds!'

'Good God, as much as that!' she gasped with genuine shock. 'The walls aren't made of gold!'

'Lots of land with it!' he said quickly. He'd much rather a secret sale because of that dreadful in-law family knowing his business, while it was too late for them to throw umpteen spanners in lots of interfering works.

'Neglected land on your own say so,' she pointed out swiftly. 'Take time, effort and money to make it productive, and also, what have you done to preserve the house? The windows and doors painted? We both know how the storms and salt-laden air thrash the house in the winter gales. Have you kept it all together, David?' she challenged.

He gritted his teeth and reluctantly shook his head. She was right, and besting him again. How did she manage to do it? 'Okay, drop the

135

price to 450 English pounds!'

Louise did a rapid think. She could find the money with selling one diamond, perhaps two? And yes, she wanted the house for ardent reasons she could never explain to anyone, including herself.

'Then there'll be what's in Simon's estate. I remember Pa covered that point in his will, though I don't suppose there'll be much?'

Louise shook her head. 'Probably fifteen pounds each,' she said, her mind still buzzing with the house. 'As to the house, I can do nothing until Jack is back. A message has gone out to him so he won't be very long, I think.' And that would give her time to talk to George Falla. 'I'll be in touch within a week unless you'd like to call here then? I must go now and talk to Simon's landlady. She'll be in shock, like me!'

He took the message with unusual understanding. 'I'll let myself out,' he said, suddenly glad to get away. He had not intended to offer the house just yet, but was glad he'd done so. A sale to her would be private, which was also what he wanted. His in-laws could go to hell.

Louise saw a weepy Janet, with Sal trying to placate her, and Sam standing helplessly to one side. 'Sal, take Janet into the sitting room. Sam, a word with you.' She took him aside. 'First thing in the morning leave a message with the advocate. I must see him as quickly as

136

possible on a private matter, I'll be seeing him later on with the quarry manager but it's vital I speak to him first,' she said urgently.

Sam nodded, instant attention, ready to leap into action at any time of day and night for his wonderful missus. He took the distressed Janet into the sitting room and flashed a look at Sal, who interpreted instantly. More brandy was going to be needed even if the ladies became drunk. Anything was in order after this awful day.

Louise saw his motive and quietly agreed with it. Later, when stone cold sober and in control, she must take the back off a picture and remove two diamonds to take to George Falla.

She took a deep drink of brandy then coughed, unused to spirits at all. She eyed the bottle with a little frown.

'I had the chance to buy it cheap,' Sam hastened to explain.

Louise eyed him. 'Was the seller well into middle age, about my height, unshaven, greying hair and a Jersey man?'

Sam nodded, perplexed at the question and the stern look on her face. Janet sat quietly, Sal by her side, each consumed with the shock of Simon's death.

'Well yes, missus, that's him!'

'That bloody man!' Louise swore with passion.

Sam flinched. 'Have I done wrong, because

. . .?' and his voice rang with worry.

'Yes, but it's not your fault. You didn't know but that Silas Regnald has it in for the Penford family. It goes back many years, when my pa slogged him one in an altercation. His downfall was witnessed by his ketch's crew, and you know how bitchy men can be. Far worse than women. Then the English excise people caught him. He went to prison for a bit. Lost everything, and not all that long ago he wanted to get Jack involved. He tried it on with me and I put my hand around his face. He tried Jack too, so he's probably crowing about selling smuggled spirits to us. I shall end up really going for him one day,' she predicted.

Sam was horrified, deeply upset, so Louise patted his shoulder. 'Don't worry. It'll come out in the wash. Now we must think of poor Simon,' she said heavily as the tears prickled again.

*   *   *

George Falla eyed her. She was bearing up well, so why this sudden urgency? Louise shook her head.

'My brother David is ready to sell his house to me!' she started, then carefully recited the conversation the siblings had held. She was careful to omit nothing, then opening her bag produced a small tube and tipped out two large diamonds. 'I have enough saved to

138

buy the house at 450 English pounds, but it is going to need doing up. Then there are going to be quarry expenses for modernisation in that direction. Can you get rid of these for me for the best price possible?'

He studied them. They were well over a carat, of good cut, colour and water. 'A wise way to use them,' he complimented her. 'Dan would approve. So do I. Leave it all with me.'

'I can't make a final decision until Jack gets back, though he knows I've always yearned to live in that house.'

'I'll start to prepare. Property conveyancing is still done in French so I'll arrange a translation for both of you. I think your brother has made a wise move to put distance between himself and his in-laws. They are a peculiar lot with more money than they know what to do with. He might end up much happier in England, and will be able buy a house there, though prices will be higher than here, as he'll find out! Should get work easily enough because he's quite well thought of in finance.'

'Do I need to sell another diamond?'

He shook his head firmly. 'Keep the others for a real rainy day. Your quarry shares can be used just for that, and don't forget, you'll have money from selling your town house.'

'That manager with the name Smythe, that's no island name!'

He nodded. 'True, English through and

through, but frustrated with the previous owners!' he told her with a twinkle in his eyes.

'But I could not have anything to do with it when I wasn't an equal shareholder, especially with a downright stranger,' she replied quickly. 'And Simon!'

'We'll talk about him tomorrow when Smythe is here, though I have a suspicion it was a pure accident due to Simon's poor understanding. Go home now. Come in the morning for a quarry meeting. Your Jack might be home quicker than you think. The sea is pretty calm, not much wind. Go home and calm your mind,' he advised gently. 'Try and get some sleep!'

Louise felt bereft when finally at home again. First her pa, now Simon. It was strange, almost eerie, in that Jack had been so precise with Sam. She could only thank God he had been so but had he undergone some weird foreboding?

Later that day, after roaming around, unable to settle to anything positive, Sam came to her.

'Missus, I've spoken to Janet about my friend, and she's going to meet him, see what he wants in the way of accommodation and meals,' and he grinned. When she sat or even stood in a certain way she was indeed a replica of her father. He had only met him a couple of times but had been impressed with his powerful character. His daughter, his missus, was very much a chip off the same block.

'Hark! That's the front door opening—can it mean . . .?' she gasped with hope, then Jack strode in, grabbed her in his arms and held her.

'My! You've made good time!' she cried, then suddenly burst into tears again.

'Delayed shock!' Jack told himself and hugged her again before leading her to the sofa. He threw a look at Sam who was preparing to remove himself discreetly from their presence. 'A hot drink and a couple of sandwiches would go down a treat!' Then he turned back to his wife. 'Tell me all as it happened and as you know it,' he told her gently. He listened with gravity then shook his head seriously.

'This might be nothing but a ghastly accident because of Simon's limited wits,' he murmured. 'You'll be meeting with your partner and this manager quickly,' he guessed.

Louise nodded, wiping her face with one hand. 'In the morning though. The coroner has already been notified.'

'So nothing can be done until then,' he said smoothly, 'and we'll try not to keep thinking about it.'

'There's more,' Louise told him, propped on his chest. 'David is willing to sell the house at Cobo Bay to me. He plans to clear off from the island and live in England with his family. Let me explain,' and she began another, even longer story, blessing her excellent memory for words and details.

Jack chewed a meat sandwich, took a drink of tea and considered. How she had yearned for that house, for reasons that puzzled him somewhat. A house was a house was a house to him, but Louise had always set such huge store upon this one.

'It's okay with me,' he hastened to reassure her quickly, pleased to see a sparkle re-enter her eyes—she was his girl of old again. 'I have always berthed my smack at St Sampson's harbour, and it's no big deal to go across country from Cobo.'

Louise emitted a huge sigh of relief. If he had objected she would have been distraught with disappointment. 'I hoped you would understand,' she said softly. 'I know you think I'm a bit crazy over one house but—I can't explain it even to myself. I was always at ease there and I love Cobo Bay and the walk up to the Grandes Rocques.'

'Then get it and let Falla do the necessary and we'll sell this once we have the other place, but say nothing to Sam or anyone until we are sure,' he advised.

'I'll just let him know you're back and give him a nod,' she agreed. 'He'll know what I mean!'

* * *

She did, and Falla did as well, flashing her just a tiny nod, indicating a chair, while Smythe stood very uncertainly. He was not used to doing business with any female and felt distinctly uncomfortable. On the basis of attack being the best form of defence he decided to have his say first. 'Simon was very good with the horses, then someone must have told him about small steam engines and he wanted to drive one. I must say, although it took him a little while to grasp it all, he became good and skilled. What he obviously never realised was that boilers, under constant hot pressure, get thin. They cannot be repaired with safety. They must be replaced. I suppose I'm to blame for not understanding his difficulty with . . .' and he paused, uncertain of the words to use.

Louise felt his embarrassment. 'Because he wasn't like us intellectually?' she suggested gently.

He nodded his relief. 'That's it exactly, ma'am.'

'It will all come out at the inquest!' the advocate said sharply to ease the sudden tension. 'But yes, stupid to hire.'

'I had been considering leaving Benson's,' Smythe said next. 'Impossible to run a quarry with the main owner absent half the time. I never knew who owned the other shares, else I'd have approached them.' His grey hair flopped untidily and his middle-aged face showed frustration.

'That was me,' Louise chipped in, 'but I didn't have a proper half share so kept out of the way of it all. Now it's totally different,' she confirmed with a firm voice.

Smythe suddenly felt a flash of hope. If only they would take a proper interest. 'As quarries go, you both know it's small but produces first-class stone, and there are years of it left to be dug out. With correct organisation from here on, the income could soar because the stone is highly valued in England.'

'Speaking for both of us,' Falla said firmly, 'let's get this quarry jumping!'

'And I second that!' Louise smiled. Before their eyes a worried, almost distraught manager was changing with relief.

He beamed at them in turn. 'It will need some capital expenditure,' he warned suddenly, soberly. 'Another crane with perfect derricks and sheer legs. Rails for both. More of those little steam engines, until the loaded stone can be taken to the ships for loading, with horses to pull the box carts. That'll speed the export up, and regular servicing of all equipment operated by steam. No more ghastly fatalities. I've always thought men work better if consideration is given to their welfare. Quarry work is extremely arduous, especially in the winter months. It's basically unhealthy work because of the silica dust, to say nothing of the sheer hard labour involved. You'll never

144

see a fat quarryman.'

'I agree with you about the men's welfare,' Louise said thoughtfully. 'Why can't some kind of portable structure be used in the bad weather? Surely the men work in little teams?'

'That's right, missus. Teams usually of five. Men who know each other well and look after each other from familiarity, even if they don't really like one another!' he grinned. This was all turning out far better than he'd dared to hope when he arose this morning and came here with reluctance.

Louise looked at George. 'I vote we leave all this to our manager as he's on the spot all the time.'

'Done, Louise. It's in your hands, manager. Just give us a weekly report, then we'll meet monthly here to mull it all over,' George told Smythe, who beamed with enormous satisfaction. He looked at his watch. 'Now I must throw you both out because I have a case in court.'

'Can I take you anywhere, ma'am?' Smythe asked politely, itching to get back to the quarry. If he gave satisfaction perhaps one day he might be allowed to buy in with a few shares for when he was a pensioner. Thank all the gods the previous male owner had been such a gambling man. England was welcome to him. His work had never been so promising.

Louise had enough natural empathy to feel his emotions and was glad the day-to-day

145

running would be left in what were, surely, competent hands. If only there had not been the tragedy of poor Simon. She suspected there might be rebuking words for Smythe from the coroner, but knowing Simon's poor IQ, as she did only so well, Smythe's only real mistake had been in not investigating this more thoroughly, with the very subject tricky to bring up. She would miss Simon so much, but it was not meant to be. Just as it had been fated for Pa to go as he did. Two sad deaths. But she would overcome, she vowed to herself, no matter what.

Then she was home and bounded into the hall for Jack. 'How did your board meeting go?' he asked as he poured her a cup of tea.

Louise once more told her story with detail and gusto, omitting nothing, not even others' thoughts. He listened intently, especially to those relating to Simon. Shaking his head he offered the biscuit plate. 'I can see the logic in your deductions. Once the funeral is over we'd better get cracking with the move. I'm sure David will want to be off the island as soon as possible. We can get this place sold, and I think we should have a word with Sam and Sal and put them in the picture. May change their plans,' he said thoughtfully. He stood, opened the door and bellowed.

Within a minute Sam strode into the room, and they both realised he had grown into a splendid young man. He would never be

146

greatly tall but his shoulders were broad and strong. He kept himself clean-shaven and always appeared well scrubbed. Sam Mahy was someone to be proud of. His family were utterly stupid.

'Sir?'

'Sit, Sam. Now tell me, have you and Sal found a place that takes your fancy yet?'

'We can't make up our minds between two town cottages, sir.'

Jack grunted. It was as he had guessed. 'Hold back a while because we are moving in the near future, though this is not to be common knowledge until we say. We shall be moving to the Castel parish, which means you may want to live there, nearer to work.'

'Oh!' was all Sam could manage initially. 'For good, sir?'

'Very much so, Sam!' Louise confirmed. 'It's my old family home at Cobo Bay, where I've always yearned to live—but don't ask me why because I just do not know!' Louise laughed. 'Do you know this parish at all?'

'No, missus, I don't, and I doubt Sal does either, but we'll go out this Sunday and snoop around,' he told them, suddenly infected with their obvious enthusiasm.

'There are ten vergées of land, which I think has been completely neglected. We'd want you to make this productive with cows, whether for milk or meat. We'd have to investigate once the land has been sorted out. Interested,

Sam?' Louise asked.

'Very much so, missus, and in this case we should live in the same parish,' Sam replied thoughtfully, his mind buzzing.

'Then you'll get a pay rise to become our foreman,' Jack chipped in.

Sam beamed with delight, and for the umpteenth time blessed the stone that had so fortunately lodged in a horseshoe.

'There's someone at the door!' he said, eager to let in the visitor and rush down to tell Sal the latest news.

Jack guessed who it had to be. 'Hello, David!'

'Not stopping. Just popped in to let you know I have instructed my advocate to get cracking,' he explained with a smile.

'When do you want to move, David?' Louise asked.

He pulled a face. 'Like yesterday?' was a sardonic reply, then he faced his sister. 'I know we've often not seen eye to eye,' he began again, 'and most of it was my fault, for which I'm deeply sorry. But there are only the two of us left now,' and he paused to marshal the correct words. 'I'd like to make up properly and once a year I'd like to spend a few days with you. Without my tribe,' he added hastily.

Now it was Louise's turn to collect her wits. She had never wholly trusted brother David, but neither had she ever heard such an admission from him before. He seemed

148

genuine, and thoughts raced through her mind. There was nothing he could do to hurt her, and it was true what he said. Just the two of them left. Would she tell him one day how her pa had really died? It was possible, but not yet.

'Let's start afresh then, brother!' she offered with a gentle smile, which was far from false.

He bent forward, kissed her cheek and hugged her. 'I thought you'd tell me to take a running jump. Bless you, sis!' and he grinned at his brother-in-law. 'Best get back home. There's uproar in the place. What to ship.What to leave behind. What to pass to the in-laws!' and he rolled his eyes almost helplessly.

Jack escorted him to the door. 'I'm being genuine,' he told Jack in a low voice. 'No tricks, no nonsense. For the first time I understand what a fine person my sister is and how like our pa she looks. Almost scary!'

Jack saw him off then returned to Louise. 'He's all right deep down. He's just had to do some belated learning!'

'So, we'd better start thinking about our proposed move as well. Let's get sorted out before I sail again!'

EIGHT

Jack had said not one word but thought a lot. Gradually though the emotional hurt had diminished and now he truly understood personally because he too had his secret.

He knew exactly her pa's estate, which was handled according to his will, and he also had a shrewd idea that the work Danny Penford had done would pay handsomely, because of the risk factor. What better way to take remuneration than in precious stones? Easily transported, hidden and never a problem redeeming for hard cash. Louise had always been his favourite, trustworthy, reliable and very close lipped. He had made her his personal repository, yet she had never confided in him. It had taken a few miles walking to reach these conclusions, and he had been left bitterly hurt. They were not just husband and wife, but pals!

She would find out his secret, one day. When that would be he had no idea. What exactly would happen to reveal the secret he did not know. He did know she was tough. She was indeed her father's daughter, and would face four square whatever life threw at her. That was just as well, he mused to himself.

'Picture,' he said to her abruptly. 'I take it you know the great French painter, the impressionist Renoir, visited us here and lived in town at number 4 George Road, St Peter Port?'

'No! I did not! Goodness me, we get famous people here even though we're only a little island. Queen Victoria visited ages ago. Look at Victor Hugo. They say he wrote his great work *Les Miserables* when here, and I intend to read this book when it's in English,' she replied, interested in this new celebrity proposing to stay.

'I don't know how many pictures Renoir painted,' Jack continued, 'nor how large, but it might be an investment to purchase one. I hear he liked natural scenes of the bays and beaches. I would like one for our sitting room, as you refuse to move your paintings from your pa!' he told her just a bit sternly.

'My pictures! My room!' Louise shot back at him feeling her hackles lift a little. She often wondered if she should confide in him what was hidden in those pictures, but something had always stayed her tongue, even though she adored him. 'Get one when available!'

Jack simply nodded. He would if he could. Now it was time to change the subject. 'Just to think, Philip marries next week!'

'Time doesn't march, it flies!' Louise agreed. 'After all, look at us! We are well into our forties now, and Sam is in his thirties. Christine is eleven and can be the most exasperating little madam!' she groaned. 'She

151

will argue so. As you know I had a horrid relationship with my mother and now I seem to be at loggerheads with our daughter.'

'We've bred ourselves a beauty though!'

'That's half the problem. She knows she has stunning looks. The boys all ogle her. She's totally uninterested in anything that doesn't relate to physical looks and beauty. She probably regards me as an old hag!'

'I'm sure you can handle one eleven-year-old, wife! Now I gather Sam has gone for Guernsey cattle for meat production?'

Louise nodded briskly. 'He pointed out milking cows are more labour intensive. You need a building for milking parlour and twice-a-day milking, as well as the milk deliveries. After all, we're not a farm, we just have land to be utilised.'

'He's quite right. Thank goodness we have him!' Jack replied, nodding with satisfaction. Also it meant Sam was always out and about on their place and lived very near in a cottage he had bought in the same parish at Castel. A very comforting thought for when he was away at sea.

'While you were away I had a flying visit from David!' 'You did? I like him, you know!'

Louise considered that for a moment. 'I must admit I do now. He's so changed! Lost all the world's worries he was carrying on his shoulders and is happy. He only stayed a couple of days. It's so simple to come over now from Southampton by steamer. I think he's being nosy, wanting to see what we'd done here and even appeared impressed. He's settled and happy in England. Good job and house and his wife and girls appear to have become more English than the English!'

'Keep in touch with him,' he advised firmly. 'He is your only blood relative from long ago,' and Jack knew exactly why he was saying this, but his expression was quite bland and gave nothing away. 'Now on to our Philip!'

'He's turned out fine, though rather young to marry!'

Jack laughed. 'You can talk!' he teased as they both went back down the years. 'Though I must admit I was surprised he went in for horticulture, but he can persuade plants to grow, especially flowers like freesias!'

'It won't be long before we'll be exporting them to England, plus our tomatoes. Our island is set to boom with a vengeance! Look how we've gone ahead with transport here! Trams and a railway coming between town and St Sampsons, and there is talk of a postal service opening as well as telephones. We shall soon leave England behind!'

'You only went there once!'

'I hated it!' Louise told him fervently. 'Too many people. Too much noise from too many horses and carriages and too far from the sea for my taste!'

He grinned. 'You're certainly island born

153

and bred, wife!'

Louise changed the subject. 'I see from your wages bill that old man from your crew has retired at last. You just have a boy to bring on and one other young fellow. Is that enough?'

'With me, and being steam now—yes! The boy is just that. Young lad keen on learning seamanship. The other is in his late twenties— le Cromier. I suppose you could call him my bosun,' he reflected before continuing. 'Been on one of the tiny fishers, but has ambition and talked himself into working for us when the old man retired. He's all right, too.'

'Le Cromier is a genuine Guernsey name, but—it's unusual with us,' Louise mused. 'Plus the common knowledge we pay well with a bonus!'

'Can Christine shine at anything, Louise?'

'Yes—arguing with me. Seriously though, she's mad about fashion and design and I must admit has good taste. Anything unconnected with this does not interest her, so she doesn't try at other lessons, stupid girl!'

Jack decided this one was the mother's problem to handle. In one way he even felt a strong twinge of sympathy for Christine up against the powerfully willed and pugnacious character of his Louise. It was this alone, he decided, that had convinced him his secret must be kept from his wife despite adoring her as he did. He knew, in his bones, her pa would have agreed too.

'And tomorrow our son marries his Jean. She's a decent island girl from a reputable family.'

'Honestly, wife,' he teased her. 'You set such store upon good breeding and the honour of the family name. I never thought about such when single. Neither did my humble family!'

'Pedigree does matter!' Louise shot back at him. There were times when their thoughts were poles apart, yet they never quarrelled. They were too close for that. Each prepared to accept the other's differing point of view. It was because of their closeness she had often rebuked herself for not telling him about her pa's hidden diamonds. Somehow she just knew she could not, even after all these years together. She realised his sharp empathy had warned Jack she had a secret, but not once had he attempted to probe. And now, she realised, she was hoist by her own petard, because Jack had some peculiar secret of his own. There were odd times when, though together, he was on another mental plane, from which she was totally excluded. Initially this had irked, then amused and finally puzzled her, but she had no intention either of probing. He would not beat her at that game!

Two days later they saw the bridal couple off. 'Well,' Jack commented, 'I thought they'd go over to England instead of planning to visit all the islands walking. Alderney, Sark, Herm and even Lithou!'

'England will come later, so Philip told me!' and she grinned. 'I supposed now it's time for you to be after your mistress once more?'

'Too right, and I have even had a hint—"when do we sail, master?" Must be short of money!' he chuckled, 'so I'll be off tomorrow. Wind's only about force three so it'll be positively gentle out there. Back in roughly a week or ten days, depending on the fish!'

Louise saw him off, had another argument with Christine over something trivial, and decided her daughter enjoyed the cut and thrust of such debates almost as a hobby. At least she never lost her temper or flew into a sulk when bested by her mother's greater knowledge. Louise had to admit to herself she even enjoyed the lead-up to such conversations, often a bit surprised at Christine's logic. Still a bit one sided at times, but she expressed herself neatly and only lost out through juvenile inexperience.

One afternoon, fairly early, while Christine was at school and Sam was working outside, her door knocker sounded briskly. She was not expecting anyone and, opening the door, she looked blankly at the young man who faced her—a total stranger and, from his clothing, a fisherman.

The stranger looked at her, his expression haggard. He went to speak, stuttered with obvious emotion and lifted both hands helplessly.

Louise went rigid and felt something clutch at her heart. She had the most horrific feeling of déjà vu. 'What is it? Where's my Jack?' she asked with a tremulous voice, almost in a whisper.

'Madame Noyen?' he asked with a catch in his voice and a pale face underneath the normal ruddy tan of one who worked out of doors in the sea air. 'I'm—le Cromier. I have to tell you—oh my God, how do I say it? It's the master, your husband . . .'

'Where is my Jack? What has happened? Has he been hurt?'

'It's worse than that, madam. As bad as it can ever get. Your husband is—dead!' he managed to splutter out at last.

Louise became a statue. Frozen in time and space. His words heard but not yet understood. She could only stare in total silence, then gradually the awful words started to penetrate. She continued to stand, motionless, speechless, helpless.

'Madam, let me call someone, anyone!'

'I don't believe it!'

'I'm afraid it's horribly true. I sailed back as fast as me and the boy could. Tied up. Saw the parish constable who arranged . . .' and his voice broke again.

'Dead? Jack, dead?' Louise could only parrot.

'Oh, madam! Let me get someone, please!'

Louise flogged her wits into action. 'My son

157

Philip was only married a few days ago, but should be back at work now. My foreman Sam is . . .' and she waved a hand vaguely to one side.

He moved into action. Opened a door on one side and bellowed. 'Foreman!' Then he took one hand and gently led her to a nearby chair. He was at his wits' end and still in shock himself from the whole experience.

'It's not possible. Not again!' Louise grated. Jack—gone? Dear God, what on earth had happened? 'Tell me! All! Hold nothing back!' Louise croaked.

He took a deep breath, gritted his teeth and explained. 'We'd just reached suitable fishing grounds. I went to help your husband with the nets and the boy had the con. Quite suddenly, out of the blue, your husband let out a cry of terrible pain, clutched his chest, bent forward, straightened up against the rail then overbalanced into the sea. I kicked off my long waders, roared at the boy to cut the engine and let her drift and I went overboard. I splashed in just yards from your husband and grabbed him, lifted his face from the water, but, ma'am, he had—gone. I knew right away because his eyes rolled back into his head. I managed to get a rope around him to bring him aboard, then sailed as fast as I could for our harbour. The parish constable took over and told me how to find my way here!'

Louise heard him in silence, face ashen,

hands trembling as Sam appeared to overhear. He froze with shock. Threw a look at his missus and the crewman. 'I'll send for your son, missus, if he's back, and inform George Falla!' he cried and realised also what he now had to do.

In his possession was a thick envelope given to him weeks ago by his master, with the strict instructions to tell no one, and only when the day arrived give it to his wife. He had been puzzled and just asked, 'But how will I know what the day is?' Jack had replied bluntly and simply. 'You will know!' This was obviously the day, and he strode away, a solid, thickset man of complete reliability. Messages to Philip and the advocate, then—the envelope.

Louise neither heard nor saw him stride away with haste. She was deep in shocked disbelief. She sat still while the fisherman hovered, anxious to do something, but *what* he did not know exactly. He felt helpless, desperate for someone else to appear.

'I still can't take it all in,' Louise choked out in a low voice. She lifted tear-filled eyes.

He held her hand. He also was in shock.

'Where is the boat?'

'Tied up at St Sampsons in the usual place. The boy is there as well. I just did not know what else to do,' he told her sorrowfully.

Louise forced herself to think again, just as Philip appeared breathing hard in his haste. She waved a hand. 'My son. Tell him!'

She studied him. He had grown into a fine, upstanding young man. Not a replica of his father, though a little like him in looks and mannerisms. She watched him flinch with shock, then he came and took her other hand. 'You must come back to me and my wife,' he told her gently. 'You're not staying here tonight,' and now he was firm.

Then Sam reappeared, took in this new scene and gnawed his lip, then slowly handed over an envelope. It had been sealed at the rear with red wax. 'Master said I was to give you this if . . .' and he ran out of words. 'Weeks ago now, missus.'

Louise took and held it. She realised this was Jack's secret and she knew she could read it only in total privacy. 'Thank you, Sam. I'll come back with you, Philip, just for one night though. As to you—you can't go out and fish alone, just you and a boy. If you can take someone with you, sail and you'll be in charge. What will eventually happen I do not know. This is all too sudden and too raw for me to handle,' and she turned to Philip. 'Christine will be home from school shortly.'

'She comes as well. Sam, go and collect her, and you'll have to explain what's happened,' Philip said.

Christine entered her home, mind whirling, then saw her mother had been crying. For the first time in her eleven years Christine had a traumatic shock. 'Dad—dead?' It was her

160

mother's tears that truly affected her. It was impossible for her mother to cry. Argue, row, tell her off—but cry? She had adored her dad. He never argued with her. He'd just listen quite gravely to her opinion, smile, chuck her under her chin and that always terminated the conversation. Mother was much more fun to row with, even if she did get verbally beaten so often. 'Dead?' she asked with disbelief.

She faced her mother and brother. A gorgeously beautiful, perfectly proportioned young female. Louise nodded, able to muster few words. 'We're spending the night at your brother's,' she explained, 'and I'll not tolerate any nonsense from you either. I've lost my beloved Jack!' and her voice broke with her sorrow and shock.

Philip lashed a warning look at his young sister and now realisation firmly set in and Christine's tears started. Her wonderful dad, gone?

It was only just before midnight, in a small solitary room, that Louise took the envelope. Philip and his wife Jean had tactfully placed Christine in with them. Philip had noted Sam hand over a heavily sealed envelope. Louise would wish to be quite alone and uninterrupted.

She opened it, angled her chair to the window, took a very deep breath and started to read.

My dear adorable Louise,

You will be sitting somewhere quite alone and reading this as a widow. Not as a wife anymore, sad to say. I've had a secret from you for quite a while now. You are good at keeping secrets and I don't think I do too badly either. It's this. There is something wrong with my heart. I may live this year out
or perhaps even a bit longer, or I could drop dead writing this letter, so here goes with the facts.

Many weeks ago, when alone luckily, I had a sudden, violent pain in my chest, I went forward and cried out, but after some seconds it went. I didn't think much of it then, but a while later it happened once more, and this time the agonising pain lasted longer. As soon as we brought the boat in and while you were at a quarry board meeting I consulted our doctor. He gave me a thorough medical and said it was my heart and there was nothing medical science could do. The first two were simple heart attack warnings and he told me the next would most likely be fatal. I was taken aback at my age, but he said some people could have heart attacks in their twenties. So

162

in a way I've been forewarned indeed. I may have days to live or only a couple of weeks.

What I do know is this. Much as I adore you, Louise, and have from the moment I spoke to your pa about you as a young person, when it comes to the inevitable I don't want to die with you. I must be with my glorious mistress.

So that is the secret I've withheld from you for a while. You have kept your pa's secret from me for years. I did eventually work it out. You were so hostile when I looked at the back of your pa's pictures I was puzzled. I went a long walk and slowly worked it all out. To start with I was deeply hurt, but keeping secrets is as natural as breathing to you. The bottom of one picture had been opened for a stone's extraction. You did not put the backing on it again to match up your pa's original. Then I slowly wondered exactly why you wanted to dispose of some. It slowly dawned on me it was at the time we bought the house, and also you and Falla wanted ready money to modernise the quarry. You had considerable savings in your account untouched in years but not enough, at that time, for everything at once, even with monies from the sale of our town house. Hence you took some of the stones, which I guess Falla handled for you. If you do anything like this again, replace the back covers like your pa did. You slipped up on that one, my darling Louise.

Now we come to our so beautiful daughter. Philip is off your hands, a man in his own right. Our girl is only that—a slip of a girl. Take my advice and cut out all these arguments with her. She only gets involved to get you going, little missy she is. You fall for it each time and I'm positive she enjoys arguing back, as a peculiar hobby. Just give a grunt, say you're too busy and walk away again. That will take the wind right out of her sails. You mark my word. After being brushed off a few times she will get your message and your life with her will be much easier.

So that's all I have to tell you, except I have never regretted one minute of my life with you. I have been honoured to have had the most wonderful experience—with you, my beloved Louise.

Your adoring Jack

At the end she was streaming uncontrollable

tears. She went back and reread the letter twice more, then folded it carefully back into its envelope. Always her skirts had been made with a deep inside pocket from the waistband. She took the skirt and carefully inserted the envelope. When she had time she would make a waterproof cover for it and always have it with her. It was even more precious than the ruby ring Jack had given her all those decades ago. This letter would always carry incalculable value to her because it was her Jack talking for the last time.

Her sleep was short, restless and miserable. Life seemed so grossly unfair to her. Most people went through their lives without having to cope with sudden death, until an aged parent died naturally. This was her third experience and the most horrific. Why her?

Philip, his wife and Christine eyed her dubiously as she appeared for breakfast. She had no appetite, so forced her toast down.

'Philip, Jean, I go home today. I can't put off the inevitable, and anyhow my lawyer will be calling, if I know him,' she told them.

'What about Pa's fishing boat?' Philip asked gently. He did not like the idea of her going home, but his mother's face now wore its inflexible look and he knew better than to comment. Thank God she would have Sam around.

'Christine, you stay here for a week until after the funeral,' Louise stated and gave her daughter a firm look, daring her to argue.

Christine was beyond that at the moment. It was her first experience of a close death and she could not stop crying her misery and shock. She liked her brother and his wife, she was comfortable with them. She also suspected her mother's grief, deeper than hers, was something to be avoided. There were times when she could be overpowering. She suddenly palled at the very thought of arguments with her. Her wonderful dad, dead!

'I'll think about it, Philip, after I've talked to the advocate,' she replied, quite calmly, even though her stomach suffered the turmoil of shock and agony. Her life was fated to go on, she reminded herself. She turned to her daughter. 'You are young for your first funeral, so if you don't wish to attend I understand. However, if you do turn up you will act with dignity. No sobbing or wailing. Jack would not approve. Neither would I,' and she flashed a warning look at Philip. He replied with a brief understanding nod. 'Get someone to take me home. I have matters to arrange.'

At home she went straight to her private office and lifted down one painting and scrutinised its rear. She certainly had slipped up. Thank goodness Jack had spotted this. She heard Sam at the open door.

'I want this room securing, Sam. Can you attend to it for me, please?'

He studied the door's solidity. 'Best thing,

166

missus, is for me to get in a locksmith. A padlock and chain would be crude,' Sam advised her.

'Good, like yesterday, please, Sam. There are to be three keys. One I will hold. The second is to go on your key holder, and the advocate will hold the third. No one is to enter here without my specific consent, unless you think there is an emergency!' she told him in a flat voice tinged with hardness.

Sam nodded. Nothing the lady did ever threw him. Over the years he had learned she always had a good reason for her actions, even when he did not understand them personally. Now she was a widow he felt huge personal responsibility for her, and this recent loss was heartbreaking for him. Jack Noyen had been a very decent bloke.

'I'll get on to it straightaway, missus,' he promised, then tilted his head as the door knocker sounded. He came back to her but not alone.

'Louise! I came as soon as I could!' It was George Falla, who pulled a chair alongside so he could hold her hand. 'I could hardly take it in. What turmoil, grief and shock for you!'

Louise felt her eyes filling once more as she related the entire ghastly event. Then she carefully extracted the envelope from its hidden pocket.

'Read it, George. No one else ever will and you will understand everything from past

167

events with Pa,' she said in a heavy voice.

He took his time, shook his head a few times then finished with a deep sigh. 'I knew Jack was smart,' he began slowly, 'but he did extra well to work it all out for himself. You're right. No one else must ever read this,' and he waved the pages gently in the air. 'It could still be dynamite for others still living.'

'I had intended to carry it with me at all times hidden in my skirt pocket, but perhaps it had better go in your safe?' Louise asked him.

'Yes, more secure with me, and you can always come in to read it whenever you want,' he replied gently. 'Jack just does not write in this letter. He talks to you!'

'Why does this always happen to me, George? This is the third time I've had this ghastly experience, but this is the very worst.' Her voice was breaking.

'I cannot answer you, Louise. I'm simply not wise enough,' and he shook his head with a sorrowful sigh.

'There's Jack's fishing smack. I want to get rid of it. As quickly as possible.'

'Don't do anything in a hurry, Louise!'

'I don't even want to see it, let alone have any connection with it,' and her tone was adamant. 'I'll speak to the crewman who has taken her out, but I know nothing about his financial situation. It might be poor,' Louise added, gritting her teeth with a frown. 'Oh Jack!' she cried silently.

168

'He could get a loan if he could rustle up a little security,' Falla added thoughtfully. Of course she'd now hate the fishing smack and she had plenty to do with Benson's accounts and considerable paperwork.

Louise left it to him. She knew she would be unable to think straight until after Jack's funeral. This was the most sombre day of her life. She watched the coffin being lowered, her heart breaking, then she took a deep breath, took a handful of soil and threw it on the coffin. She gave Christine a nudge and rested one hand on the girl's shoulder. She had behaved admirably for someone of her years, and she could sense Philip and Jeans' influence, for which she was grateful. She turned once, looked back again then walked from the cemetery. It was the finite end of this part of her life. No matter how long she was destined to live she was positive nothing, no action, no unexpected future event, could ever break her heart like these dreadful two weeks. A good part of her was being smothered by the gravediggers, who were throwing soil on the coffin lid.

'Home!' she told them all bleakly.

NINE

Louise passed through the next few weeks almost automatically. She attended to her tasks but her aching heart, with its great void, was in constant pain. She accepted, in one way, she was better off than other wives suddenly widowed. All of her life with Jack had been nothing but a succession of comings and goings because of his work. Over these years of her adorable marriage to him, she had worked out a routine that suited her temperament. In a queer way she was, thus, in part able to accept he was no longer around. No more coming home smelling of fish, craving good red meat with onion gravy followed by fruit pie and cream. She struggled to pretend he was simply away at sea again. The nights were the worst when realisation of her position would hammer at her sore heart, and on those nights her pillow was constantly wet from unstoppable tears.

Christine had altered as well, which was disconcerting.

She made no attempt to involve her mother in arguments. It was as if she had retreated into an unbreakable shell, and Louise was forced to accept Jack's death had had a traumatic effect upon an eleven-year-old girl. She tried to talk to her gently but any response was sluggish, if one came at all. Mostly Christine would simply shrug her shoulders and wander off. This was so out of character it became another worry, but both Philip and Jean advised her not to make an issue of it. Let her work it out of her system in her own way. She was still so young.0

Then there was Derek. He came back from his fishing trip, brimming with enthusiasm for the catch with the boy and another man. Louise listened to him, then took him to one side where they were private.

'I'm finishing with this business,' she told him gently. 'This is no reflection on you,' she added, seeing his eyes narrow with shock and disappointment. 'It's just I cannot have anything now to do with fishing. I'm going to sell Jack's smack. Do you want first refusal, Derek?'

She had no intention of telling him the income was no longer necessary. She and her partner were doing splendidly with Benson's quarry. And there was a huge amount of paperwork now involved, which just about made her a full-time worker in this field. She had carefully gone over the quarry's figures, which with increased yield through Ernie's good management now produced an income anyone would be comfortable with.

In many ways Jack's fishing had become a sideline in comparison, and she knew he would have been the first to agree.

She looked at Derek. She had given him the most enormous shock. He had returned to port, delighted with this first catch, but his heart now sank.

'There is nothing I'd like more than to buy, ma'am, but I don't have that kind of money. I'm just an ordinary struggling family man. We've always lived from one pay packet to the next,' he told her heavily.

Louise thought quickly. Derek le Cromier must be all right, or else Jack would never have engaged him as a crewman. 'There is more to it than plain fishing,' she explained slowly. She felt an urge to help him because he was a link with darling Jack. 'Someone has to keep accounts and records, arrange payment of wages to the crew, and a bonus when the catch is right. Do you know anyone who could handle this for you?'

He felt a tiny flare of hope. 'Why yes, ma'am. My wife could!'

Louise nodded. 'Good! It pays to keep private matters in the family. My affairs are handled by the advocate George Falla. I'll have a word with him, hopefully in the morning. And then let you know. Incidentally there is a Jersey man who may try to involve you in smuggling. His name is Silas Regnald. Don't fall for his smooth talking. He is trouble through and through, and he dislikes me immensely and my family. It all goes back decades to my long dead pa. Years ago he lost

172

his ketch and was caught by the English Excise. He's a disaster.'

Derek blinked. 'I've already spoken to him! He met me at the harbour with a smooth line in patter but I'm no fool, ma'am. Like others I know what went on here, but I'm simply not interested,' and his tone was firm.

Louise believed him. Jack would have too. 'I'll be in touch within forty-eight hours, so stay handy.'

With that she saw him depart and took a deep breath. George would have some idea, she knew, and tomorrow she'd be at his office. She'd already made some decisions. Seamen could, she knew, be highly superstitious. Better Derek have the smack, and a fresh outlook? Easier to say she'd gone down in a squall, which was never unusual. The boy would not understand and in years to come that would be how she'd describe Jack's death. Derek would start with a clean sheet, fresh name and fishing smack. It was the same with her pa's and ma's deaths. Only Falla knew the whole truth. There were enough gossipy tongues on the island without handing out unnecessary fodder for them. If anything happened to Philip, God forbid, she would consider him to have gone likewise. Death at sea was so commonplace here it was allowed to pass without comment.

She saw the advocate the next day and explained her logic. George Falla thought she was now inclined to go over the top, but let it ride because it was true, island tongues could wag.

'No problem in transferring the smack's ownership to le Cromier, but what about payments for her, Louise?'

'Monthly instalments?' she suggested.

'No problem if you're happy, though it will take time,' he pointed out.

Louise nodded. 'I can afford that now we're getting such a good income from the quarry.'

'Send him to make an appointment to see me and I'll sort it all out. It's true. The quarry is doing very well now, with no end in sight according to Ernie—England can't get enough of our stone. Fantastic market for us,' he mused, then realised her eyes were on him, eloquent and asking. Without a word, he went to his safe, opened it and handed her the envelope. She sat quietly reading as he watched the emotions play over her face.

'Jack's talking to me again!' she murmured with a catch in her throat. She had a prickle at the back of her eyes and sniffed deeply. Holding the envelope and pages brought him back to her each time, and finally slipping the precious pages back she returned the envelope to her legal friend with a watery smile.

*   *   *

He studied the fisherman before him, who sat very uncomfortably facing his chair—quite out of his element in a legal office, his body language almost shrieking. Falla studied him carefully. He had made a few discreet personal enquiries and knew this man was solid and reliable. It was possible he was not extra-bright, but in a storm he knew anyone would be very safe with him. But not fish. He was a natural fisherman with a sharp nose for finding them. His domestic life was sound. He did not have a loose tongue. Excellent citizen, and it would be both a duty and pleasure to assist him.

'You understand me? It's madam's express wish that her husband's smack overturned and he died at sea that way.'

'Yes, sir, and anyhow she nearly did overturn. There was just a very green boy at the wheel. When I went in she canted to one side, and I thought she was going over. Especially when I dragged the master back aboard, she nearly went over once more. Don't know how she kept upright.'

'Also you are to change her name and repaint her. You have steam, so remove that mast now and the smack's whole appearance alters.'

He nodded, still bemused with it all. 'But that Jersey man approached me and—'

'The smuggler? Don't touch him with a bargepole, and tell him nothing. As far as anyone's concerned you've acquired an unexpected benefactor and it's no one's business!' George said harshly. 'You are just carrying out madam's wishes. You'll pay quarterly to my office and receive a statement from me ditto. Understand?'

'Yes sir!'

'And acquire tight lips!' he warned.

Derek was too bemused by it all to argue. He had never envisaged owning his own fishing smack. It was just about impossible to take in his luck and his gratitude for Madame Noyen was boundless, as well as for this big advocate, Falla of the States of Deliberation. He could merely shake his head and smile his thanks as he stood. Why Madame Noyen wanted this situation was beyond him but he would always be her devoted slave.

Later on, when Louise had received a written report from George she turned to Sam and pointed at a thin packet she'd brought in. 'Get that hung, Sam, please. In my sitting room facing Jack's chair. It is a Renoir and only a smallish one but it pleases me and they say his work will increase in value in due course. Probably when he's dead though.' she mused.

Sam studied the painting and nodded approvingly. 'Surely that is Moulin Huet, if I know my island. Lovely colours and composition.'

Louise's eyebrows shot up. 'Didn't know you had feelings about art, Sam?' she asked with a smile.

'Not a lot, missus. I either like or dislike what I see. This I like!'

*　　*　　*

Now here she was, years later, Louise reminded herself. At the end of this year she would have reached her half-century, and at this year's end they would enter another century starting with the number nineteen. Where had the years flown?

She still went to her legal friend's office to read Jack's letter, but not as often now, as it had been well memorised. There was comfort though in holding the paper pages, but she had prudently added a codicil to her will that on her demise the letter was to be burned. No one, not even her children, was to read it. It was an object incredibly private.

She smiled at Sam as he joined her in their rear garden. It was full of fresh vegetables and flowers. He had worked for her now for more years than she cared to remember, and there was good friendship between them, without undue or possessive familiarity. Each respected the other, even if they disagreed at times.

'What's it like, missus, being a grandma?' Sam asked with a twinkle in his eyes.

Louise let out a groan. 'Don't rub my age in!' she protested.

Sam laughed. 'You can't get away from

having two grandsons, missus! Philip and his Jean have done well. But as to your daughter?' and Sam rolled his eyes and shook his head. 'She changed after your husband's death, and not for the better, though she's a real stunner for her looks.'

'That's the trouble. Boys follow her everywhere, and she dotes on the power she wields over them, the fools. Once she used to argue black was red and nearly drive me mad, but now I'm lucky to get a word from her and she doesn't do as she's told, either. I've tried gentle discussion, but she's like a castle with the drawbridge well and truly up. She wants to go to England, so I've told her flat she can go when she's twenty-one and not before.

I also told her if she became any more difficult I'd lodge a complaint with the parish constable, as someone out of control. That did register. Now she detests me and all of a sudden I don't give a damn. Hope your kids don't trouble you?'

Sam shook his head. He had similar feelings about Christine. She would snub him if given a chance. He had a nasty idea she was going to turn into a bad one. Total opposite of Philip, who had not given five minutes of trouble all his life. Kids! Were they worth having, he pondered?

'David hasn't been over for a bit,' he commented, well aware he was on a fishing trip for gossip. 'I often puzzled why he didn't

178

appear for the master's funeral.'

Louise knew his tactics of old, which always amused her. 'I must admit I was hurt that he never turned up, but when he did I understood. He was away in London on a longish business trip, so never received George's letter until he returned, which was on the day of the funeral. When he did get back he was infuriated to discover the Guernsey in-laws had turned up just about en masse. His wife and daughters were likewise not enthusiastic. Wild horses would not drive any of them back to an island life, so said in-laws decamped after a shortish visit and have never been back. David said this suits all of them.'

'But he comes to see you once a year, doesn't he?'

Louise nodded. 'And I enjoy his visits too. Jack always liked him despite our rowing days. He told me David had changed suddenly—like Christine—but, with him, for the better. I enjoy having him here too,' she admitted. Once such a statement would have verged on heresy.

'I think he's all right. Not a bit stuck up. When's he coming again, do you know, missus?'

'Soon, I think, though I'll have my hands a bit full. You see Philip and Jean have always wanted to visit England, especially London. They've asked me to look after Charles and Duret for them. Jean's parents are not in good health and are unable to cope with a lively pair of boys, even if they are still so young. And Janet is now far too old and frail, so if I don't have them they won't be able to go.'

'They are a splendid pair with healthy kids. This house is large enough with all these vergées for them to explore and play in. I could always keep a watchful eye, if you wished to go out at any time,' he offered sincerely.

'Sam, that would be splendid, though getting out and about here is so simple now. Electric trams, the railway from St Sampsons to St Peter Port. The telephone. A postal service. We're every bit as modern as England!'

'To say nothing of our island trade!' Sam added. 'Anyhow that's settled re the grandkids! When do they plan to go, missus?'

'They want to be back for Easter, and they've booked their return passage on the *Stella*, sailing from Southampton, so they'll have about two weeks over there to explore,' Louise explained. 'By which time I'll no doubt have acquired grey hairs,' she chuckled.

Sam was pleased. A long time ago he had wondered if she would ever smile again, let alone manage to chuckle Jack's death had been a hammer blow in the dark, and until after the funeral she had been preoccupied with sorting out legal affairs, working with the advocate.

He did not agree with all she did, but it was

180

hardly his place to comment He noticed even Philip had little to say to her, while Christine said noting at all. She was certainly no doting daughter, and it had crossed his mind that her father's sudden death may have affected her mentally. On the other hand, until then, had she shown true affection for her mother? Not once.

Christine was only truly interested in one person. Christine. She had been glad to leave school with an acid report, to the effect she could have done better. Her work now was, in his eyes, trivial rubbish. Fashion!

'I'm going to see George,' Louise told him, interrupting these morbid thoughts. 'It wouldn't surprise me to see David bounding in some time.'

'Going on your trike, missus?'

She grinned. 'Yes, I am. I still get raised eyebrows, even though we have such excellent transport today—pedalling is such great fun to me! It's a decent refreshing ride from Cobo too.'

It was not long afterwards she sat with George Falla in his office in what she called her particular chair.

He went to his safe, extracted the envelope, passed it to her, then sat back, watching her. She was fifty this year—incredible to think she had come to him as an eighteen-year-old. He remembered how horrified he had been when Dan arranged their first meeting, and

181

how matters had escalated since then in ways impossible to envisage at the time.

Now he considered himself her uncle and was always pleased to see her, though she could be a handful at times, with a pugnacious streak and a steel backbone. How well she had coped with what life had thrown at her, not least her father's horrific murder. When she had first hurled that at him he'd wondered if the shock had upset her mental equilibrium.

Like all good men of law he had appropriate contacts. A discreet investigation into circumstances, the few facts available and a detailed knowledge of human nature, and jealousy as well as plain old-fashioned gossip, had shown Louise was correct. Nothing could be done, of course.

Then there had been Simon's death, quite out of the blue. Finally the loss of her beloved and much adored Jack. She had risen above all these disasters and shocks in a manner that filled him with pride. It was true, she was Dan Penford all over again. Not just in looks, but in mannerisms, temperament, intelligence, and, in certain stances, she was almost his double. Enough to be uncanny! He knew breeding could produce strange results. Perhaps she might have a grandchild who was a Penford through and through, before showing as a Noyen.

Louise was aware she was under his detailed scrutiny. She grinned at him. 'Do I pass muster?' she cheeked.

'I suppose so,' he shot back at her quickly. 'What do our accounts say?'

Louise, now serious, pulled from her bag neatly handwritten notes and accounts. 'We are doing very well. Great demand for dressed stone for buildings and also for aggregate. The latter of course is easier to ship. Just tip it into the ship's holds and a ship can be in and out in one day, and it's certainly more convenient at St Sampsons. Takes longer of course to handle and load the dressed stone, but the demand for such is non-stop. Horses pulling the carts often have to wait in a queue, but it's very well organised. At this rate we're going to end up just about rich!'

'Do you still want me to invest for you?'

'Yes, George. Same as before. Half to invest for the highest safe interest. The other half of my share also to get interest, at a lower rate, I know—I'll always need cash for wages and living expenses and money in my purse.'

'I do pretty near the same, and also invest my legal earnings in a similar way. You're fifty this year. I am sixty and I intend to retire from the States at sixty-five. Let fresh younger blood take over.' And he noted her eyes narrow thoughtfully. He knew her so well and shook his head reassuringly. 'Don't fret. I'll still keep a handful of private clients, which certainly includes you. Once I retire officially you can always deal with the practice in general.'

'I don't suppose anything more will happen to me where a big legal problem will arise. I think I've had my share, enough for half a dozen lives,' she told him with a heavy and sad look on her face and in her eyes.

He nodded. 'Yes, I certainly agree with you on that one, and Dan would be proud, very proud of how you've faced everything!' he praised, and meant his words. 'There is Ernie though.'

Louise blinked, taken aback for a few seconds. She liked their quarry manager. Ernie Smythe was a fine man, though it had taken her a long time to break down their personal barrier. To Ernie, females and quarries did not mix at all, but as she was a half owner he could not ban her from the place. Certainly the men liked her visits. Her presence toned down their language and she would never hesitate to have a mug of tea and chatter to them. She asked about their families, with an interest never false—her comments were not made simply to pass the time of day. The workmen, all of them, adored her.

'What *about* Ernie?'

He gave a tiny shake to his head and frowned. 'At our last board meeting, anything strike you, Louise?'

She thought back. 'He appeared to have a bit of a cold,' she said frowning, puzzled.

'Yes, he coughed a few times and I have my suspicions. Cold, my eye! I have a very nasty feeling it might be early silica trouble with his lungs. He's spent all his working life with quarries, and although he's not had to breathe in the silica like the masons or cutters, there must still have been a risk.'

'Oh! Are you saying . . .?'

'Remember that older, ginger-haired bloke, left now? His lungs were riddled. He doesn't have long, I've heard. If Ernie's starting to . . .?'

'That's terrible!' she cried. 'I've become real fond of him!' 'I think we should both lean on him to see a doctor, then think about what we'd do if the inevitable happens.'

Louise groaned. 'Not dear Ernie!' she protested. 'But you're right. Doctor for him and no argument. Better to come from you than me, but if necessary I'll step in as backup.'

'Trouble is, he's the type who'll die happily in harness. The quarry is his life. Not too good a marriage either from bits and pieces I've picked up. But I think we should look long term. A good manager is vital. He does have a son who works in a Welsh quarry.' George told her thoughtfully

'Sound him out, George, but be tactful. Ask if his son would like to come here as Ernie's understudy for when he retires. He might accept that idea!'

'Good thinking, Louise. I'll get onto it this very week. If he pulls a face at seeing a doctor I'll tell him you'll come and you have a temper on you.'

'Really, George. Don't make me into an ogre!' she protested.

'Well you do. I can see your hackles standing erect right now, Niece!'

'Niece! If that's how you regard me, I am deeply honoured, Uncle!' Then she changed the topic. He was indeed a gorgeous uncle when she thought about it. 'I'll be a bit tied up for a little while,' and she explained about Philip and Jean going to have a break in England, and how she'd become a grandma. 'I'll have help because I'm rather out of practice with hectic toddlers round my feet. Sam's wife Sal is going to have them with hers during the day, and Polly will help at night. I shall pay both of them, so I'll carry on with our accounts, of course. My office is totally private, with a locked door at all times.'

'Still have Dan's pictures—and contents—safe?' he asked gently.

'Very much so. My reserve emergency funds, as Pa would have wished,' she assured him. 'Only us two know, and Sam also has a key, though doesn't know what for exactly, though he's far from stupid. Mind you he's not impressed with those pictures. He prefers the Renoir!'

'Wise!' he replied nodding firmly. 'Keep it like that!'

'I only went in once—to remove those two stones when buying David's house, and for money modernising the quarry.'

'You have this recorded in your will, and then, and only then, I guess, will be the time to let them see the light of day.'

Louise stood. 'I'd better get back. Philip and Jean go off in two days and it would never surprise me if David did not appear. His last visit was way before Christmas, so he's overdue as nosy parker again!' she chuckled. She read his unspoken question. 'Yes, we get on fine now. Thank goodness he went to England. He's a different and much nicer man than before!'

She hesitated outside then decided to go down to the harbour. It was packed with traffic consisting of box carts loaded with aggregate and stone to go to England. As the carts inched forward in a specific order she admired the patient horses. It was obvious they were used to this activity. When beckoned to move it was only a few paces, and their drivers would halt at a precise spot to unload into the ship's hatches. Dust flew everywhere, so she wheeled back a few strides, and turned and halted with a perplexed frown.

That was Derek, and she wished to have a rare word with him, but who was at his side? Obviously there was some kind of masculine row going on. Derek was red-faced like his companion. Her eyebrows shot up as Derek balled a fist and thrust it forward. The other man backed two steps and hurled what could

187

only be imprecations at Derek. He strode forward another step and now the other retreated sullenly and reluctantly.

Louise's frown deepened. Who was he? Why did an alarm bell ring in her mind? He was dressed in the usual hard-wearing seaman's trousers and Guernsey sweater, neither too clean. He was older than her but about her height. His hair was quite white and his shoulders were bowed, so she guessed his age to be in the early seventies. She studied the features. Not clean-shaven, hair untrimmed, angry-looking.

The man suddenly realised he was under observation, turned, studied her and glowered. Louise blinked at such blatant hostility and her temper began to fizz. Then recognition dawned with a rush. It was the old Penford family enemy, Silas Regnald.

Derek spotted her at the same time. With one hand he made a very rude gesture, then came over to her. 'Madame Noyen!' he greeted her with delight.

'Hello, Derek. He still trying it on?'

'Yes, madam. I have to admire his persistence, stupid man,' Derek growled.

'He must be hard-up, to the point of desperation. I can only presume life has become too hot for him on Jersey now. He looks as if he's one hundred and two!'

'I've told him repeatedly I'll not be a party to smuggling, putting my lovely *Susan* at risk,'

Derek explained, and pointed below to where a very smartly yellow-painted fishing smack lolled gently tied to the pier side.

'Susan?'

'I named her after my missus,' Derek told her. 'I did fancy calling her Louise but didn't think you'd approve,' he said with a bewitching grin.

Louise threw back her head and laughed. She liked this man. 'It might have been imprudent! I'd like to say, Derek, I think you did remarkably well paying off the loan as you did—I realise some months it must have been tight for you.'

'It was, madam, but me and my missus agreed it was very worthwhile. We could never have done it the normal way. No one would have given us a loan without security. We owe all to you and your generosity.'

'Oh do shut up, Derek! You're making me feel embarrassed!' Louise protested, which was true.

'No, madam. You have two slaves for life with me and Susan. If ever you need help we both hope you'll turn to us. Promise, madam?'

She looked into his kindly face, deeply touched. She did not consider she had done anything particularly remarkable. Uncle George, God bless him, had handled the transfer of ownership and the loan as well as supervising the monthly repayments. She doubted whether the person had been born who could pull a fast one over her advocate.

'I'm going back to Cobo!' she said suddenly 'But keep a beady eye on that crapaud Regnald. If he can cause trouble for me and mine—and this now includes you—he will. Always remember, Derek!'

'Not 'arf, madam!' Derek said passionately.

'Bye then. If *you* ever want assistance of any kind you know where I live, *and* the office of advocate Falla!' and she swung her trike around, mounted, settled her ridiculous long skirt comfortably and started to pedal. Would a day ever come when females could wear comfortable clothing like trousers, she wondered?

She was tired when she reached home, where Sam greeted her. 'Your son and his wife have been with your grandsons plus a mountain of toys,' he laughed. 'Might play with them myself,' he admitted with a grin.

'And I might just join you. I suppose it's too much to hope Christine has been around?'

'She had her breakfast then went striding off in the direction of town, without a word to say to anyone.'

'Damned girl!' Louise wore. 'I did offer to get her a trike but she never deigned to answer. She lives in her own peculiar world, from which I am most certainly excluded. But she earns her own money with those fashion designers, pays her own way, so I don't suppose I can grumble,' she admitted heavily.

Sam had his private opinion, but tactfully kept these thoughts to himself. How could one death, even though it was her father, so change a person's character to such an extent?

TEN

Louise beamed with genuine delight. 'David!'

'Well, it's been a long time. Way before Christmas!'

'Yes, I know. Sorry about the absence, but I've had my hands full, but it's all worked out to my satisfaction at last! Have married off my three girls, so it's just me and my wife, so hopefully my finances will be allowed to improve. There are now husbands to look after my girls' expensive tastes!'

'Well! It doesn't seem possible, the years hurtle by so fast,' she mused.

'What's all this with kids' toys?'

'Philip and Jean are having a holiday in England, so I'm being grandma good and proper, though I have help with Sam's wife and sister. I'm a bit out of practice!' she grinned.

'When are they due back?'

'On Maundy Thursday, on the train steamship *Stella*!' she told him.

'And I sail back on her for Easter at home, so this is going to be a short visit this time, sis. I'll do better next time,' he promised, and

191

meant it.

The next day she drove him out to Benson's quarry, where he stood at the rim, looking at the scene so very far below.

'The men and horses all look so tiny,' he said with awe. 'I'd never been to a quarry before. Didn't interest me, but this,' and he waved a hand expressively, 'it's amazing! Even a bit scary from this height!' he murmured to her.

Louise knew exactly how he felt. Those had been her early sentiments. He turned back to her.

'And Pa gave you your share of this when eighteen?'

She nodded and waited, sensing more questions were to come. David had his deep-thinking expression on his face.

'Once the girls were off my hands and the in-laws had all returned I found myself drifting back down the years. Especially relating to our pa. You've always been a superb secret-keeper, and it slowly dawned on me you have kept matters from me, and perhaps even your Jack?' he questioned in a low but firm voice. 'Did he know about this quarry?'

Louise smiled. 'Not for many years, and when I did tell him he nearly collapsed,' she admitted.

'But you had a good marriage with him, I know. You adored him, didn't you?' he probed again.

Louise gave a sad smile. 'I adored him and it just about broke my heart when he went so suddenly, *and* when he'd kept his illness a secret!'

'So what secret are you still keeping from your brother, your only blood kin? What exactly did happen to our pa?'

Louise thought for only a few seconds. 'Mother murdered him!' she spat out bluntly.

'She did *what*?' he gasped, horrified. 'For God's sake, sis, tell me! All!' he demanded.

So she did. The main protagonist was long dead. There had never been tangible evidence and a charge could not be laid against a killer who was paralysed by stroke and whose mind had gone.

He listened aghast. Then reflected and finally nodded his head slowly. 'It's hard to take in, but knowing both of them it does make sense. It's horrible, and yes, this stays between the two of us, because I take it Jack never knew.'

'My advocate was told but said nothing could be done to produce justice for Pa!' she said, bitterness ringing in her voice.

'It's taken me up to now to tell you, because you'd never have believed me before, would you?'

'No. Who would?' and he paused to reflect. 'What other secrets have you as well?'

'Goodness me. None!' Louise lied smoothly and stared at him blandly. 'What others could

193

I possibly have?'

He didn't know whether to believe her or not, but had enough nous not to press. The person had not yet been born who could browbeat her, and he looked carefully from the side. God, he thought, she looked the spitting image of the old man too!

Louise shivered. 'It's raw cold. Let's go home. I hope the mist will have started to lift a bit, but there's not a breath of wind so it's unlikely. Your steamer may be late in if there's mist at Southampton,' she commented thoughtfully. 'I'll come with Sam to see you off, and take the larger trap for Philip and Jean. I guess they'll have a mountain of luggage and parcels.'

Her brother was quiet that evening, sitting with little to say as he faced the Renoir. 'I find that soothing,' he said nodding at it. 'I swear I can smell the sea as well. Yet it's gentle and relaxing. I need that, after this morning,' he admitted to her.

She understood. His shock had been profound and she poured them both a brandy, a large one for him. They had no talk. None was needed, she knew. It was going to take him a long time to accept her revelation. They sat in silence, just the background noise of young children being put to bed.

'You have good staff,' he did say.

'I pay people well, so they're loyal too,' she said. 'And we've always been so lucky to have

Sam. He's the backbone of the place,' she reflected. 'He doesn't always agree with me and speaks his mind. I let him but often we simply disagree and go our respective ways Jack thought the world of him.'

'Jack was a splendid brother-in-law. I was real cut up when he died so suddenly. It must have been sheer hell for you, sis, but you rise above it all,' he complimented with sincerity.

'No good sitting moping and howling,' Louise replied in a low voice, 'though I often felt like it.'

'You've had more than your fair share of terrible disasters. Our pa would have been real proud of you—like me!' and he paused. 'How could Mother . . .?'

Jealousy, and thriving on the wrong interpretations at all times,' Louise snarled. 'How I ended up hating her, yet there was not a single thing I could do.'

'Come on, drink up, I'm leaving you behind. I'm going to need this to help me sleep,' he said slowly, already feeling the spirit's numbing effect.

That he did sleep Louise guessed was as much from intoxication. She herself had imbibed more than usual and she had felt its anaesthetic need. Opening up to her brother had brought it all back with a vengeance. She wondered what Jack would have thought. He would have been totally shocked, with disbelief to start with, but he had never known her parents properly. Gradually he too might have accepted her version of events, but she was glad now he never knew. And certainly David would never know about the precious stones and their perfect hiding place. She considered he might have some jealousy still, because of their pa always favouring her over his firstborn.

Her brother was so different now that he'd left the island. Now that his daughters were off his hands—and away from his wallet—he seemed happier and more content with his marriage.

She slept well, her thoughts gradually untangling, until she relaxed completely. David stirred late next morning, and appeared shaking his head ruefully.

'Your brandy—it's powerful!'

'Never mind. You might not do it again for ages. Now we must think of getting you ready for tomorrow,' Louise said briskly.

'The *Stella* is due to sail from Southampton at 11.40 a.m., and she's fast, she can do a good nineteen knots, so it should be a rapid sail,' he said to her.

'I bet she'll be jam-packed with people coming back for Easter,' Louise mused. 'Who is the captain, do you know, David?'

'Yes, I asked when I made the booking. It's Captain Reekes. I gather he's made this crossing often, so should know every ripple of every wave,' he smiled.

Christine entered the kitchen and forced a welcoming smile on her face. 'Hello, Uncle David!'

A new face surely was an ally? Anyone better than her mother. She knew perfectly well her attitude towards her mother had been disgraceful for years. Once it had been great fun, even entertainment, to engage her in arguments, but it had all changed when her father died so suddenly. Why, she neither knew, understood nor even cared—all she could think was her mother baulked her life.

She was so old and badly dressed. She had no idea of fashion, and wore the same dowdy clothes year in, year out. It was impossible to contemplate a discussion about fashion with her, which after all was her major interest.

But here was a man. A man who didn't come often. A new target for her ambitions? This gave her something to consider apart from her current niggling worries.

'Uncle David. I want to go to England. Fashion here is impossible, and she won't let me go until I'm twenty-one!'

David was startled momentarily. Quite taken aback at his niece's incredible beauty. He threw a look at Louise and saw she was angered and exasperated. He had not brought up three girls without learning a thing or two about their lives and behaviour. He had also developed a sense for hostile atmospheres. Quite suddenly, he felt for his sister. The horrors through which she had lived, with three deaths, and the last having left her alone.

He moved with a speed that startled mother and daughter. He stepped forward and slapped Christine's face with a hearty blow on her left cheek.

'Who the hell do you think you're referring to, "she"?' he roared at her. 'The cat's mother!' he snarled.

Christine went flying backwards and landed with a thud on her backside, gasping with shock!

'It's time you showed a bit of respect for your mother!' he continued.

Christine struggled to her feet, shocked and humiliated. 'But Uncle . . .' she tried to begin again.

'Don't but me!' David continued. He now realised his sister's hands had been over-full for a long time, and his instinct was to protect her.

'Well!' he bellowed once more.

Christine realised her error had been gross. 'I'm sorry, Uncle. Sorry, Ma,' she managed to get out, tears in a hover.

'Get yourself off to your so-called work,' Louise snapped and turned to David. 'This is what I'm having to put up with all the time. Ever since my darling Jack died. All Christine is prepared to consider is—Christine!'

'Not anymore, sis,' David grated. 'Just let me know of any more problems from her.

We're both on the telephone now, and it's easy enough to get here by rail and steamer. My three girls were brought up with respect and manners, and I'm not having you tolerate any more crass behaviour!'

Now Christine felt nothing but fear. Other, gorgeous males did not treat her like this. If —and her mind shied away from the question hidden deep in her mind . . . what if—? And she could only hope, pray and count more carefully.

'I'll get off to work then. Sorry again, Ma, Uncle David!' She left the room, shutting the door firmly then leaning against it.

'Thanks, David. That was long overdue. I never thought Jack's death would so change her. He was very easy-going with her, but would have turned eventually.'

'Trouble is, she's the most beautiful female I've ever met, and I bet she knows it too!' David said heavily.

'Not 'arf!' Louise replied inelegantly. 'The boys have always buzzed around her like wasps round an open jam pot!'

'Do as I say, sis. Any more shenanigans from her, phone me and put her on! I'll give her verbal hell and threaten to come straight over!'

'Thanks, bro! Now we'd better think of getting you down to the harbour tomorrow. I'll get Sam to use the cob with the larger trap. More space.'

Christine leaned against the door, eavesdropping. She had received a ghastly shock and been disappointed. Always before, on her Uncle David's very erratic visits, she had paid him no attention. This time though it had hit her perhaps he would come down on her side as he lived in England. He was, surely, the one person who could stand up, in Christine's opinion, to her obdurate mother, and persuade her to let her leave for England now, and not wait another tedious two years. Her mother was such a has-been, which was understandable at her great age, but her uncle had let her down.

To start with, he had not reacted to her great beauty. She could have been as dismal and plain as a pole. All other males thought she was gorgeous, and said so by word and deed. Instead he had backhanded her, and now threatened to come over, right away, on her mother's say so. This was too dreadful for contemplation. Then she might even have another problem. She had no close female friends. She realised this was because she so outshone her rivals, so what to do for the best? Grit her teeth and force herself to wait twenty-four months and carry on living at Cobo? She did not earn enough money to find lodgings for herself, yet unless she could turn her charm on some other well-heeled male she was stuck. She must bend her mind to this, she thought as she slipped away and headed for town.

The next morning Sam brought the cob around, harnessed to the largest trap.

'Nice animal!' David said as he stroked an inquisitive grey nose.

'Yes,' Louise remarked. 'He did work for the quarry pulling the carts to the harbour, but then he threw a swollen tendon. I arranged for him to come here, and Sam has nursed the leg back to normal. He's perfect for private use, but not for pulling quarry carts. He has a placid temperament, so he's joined the family permanently,' she smiled.

'I see it's still misty,' David commented thoughtfully. 'The steamer may be late in.'

'True, but I think it would be wise to get down to the harbour. Sam will have to find somewhere to park, and the place is bound to be crowded. There will be so many people arriving back for the Easter weekend, and others like you,' Louise pointed out.

The next morning, with Sam at the reins, Louise and David sat together on the front seat as they gently ambled into town. The outskirts were crowded, with everyone heading for the harbour, talking, shouting, excitable.

'What on earth is all this about?' Louise asked her brother. 'Don't ask me, unless Easter's come early. It's weird,' he replied, equally puzzled.

'Oi! You! With that cart! You can't go down to the harbour. Too many people. Park in a side street!' called a constable, red-faced

201

and worked up over something. 'Hey, you, get some help! I can't control these people alone!'

'Sam, turn up there. Tie the cob to that lamppost. We'll have to go in on foot!' Louise cried.

Sam hastily obeyed, leaped from the cart, looped the reins securely to one wheel, then releasing two straps slipped the bit from the cob's mouth, fastening a nosebag for the patient animal. The cob was delighted to get an extra breakfast and started to eat, oblivious to all this human activity.

David threw a look around. They were now part of a throng heading for the harbour. All of a sudden, he decided not to take his case. It must stay, and if stolen there was nothing of value in it. Louise nodded her agreement.

'I don't know what the hell's going on. After all, the steamer comes in regularly, with no fuss, no ado, and Easter's still a couple of days away.'

'I've never seen the like! Have you, Sam?' Sam shook his head firmly, also baffled.

David took charge. 'We must stick close together. It'd be easy to lose one another in this. When it comes time to board I'll race back and grab my bag. Now, Louise, you grab hold of my left sleeve, tightly now. Sam, take the right. Now let's go!'

David tried to march forward firmly, which was impossible with so many people, a lot of whom were now very worked up. It was hard to hear the person next to you, with all the cries and agitation of the crowd.

'Something's happened!' Louise cried in sudden fright.

Both David and Sam could see she was right, but said nothing, colluding only in their looks. With tense face and gritted teeth David struggled on, towing the other two with him, a tiny determined phalanx. Others had the same idea.

The harbour was packed and two other constables struggled to keep order. 'Passengers, wait over there! Those meeting someone, keep this side!'

There was huge activity in the water. Boats were rushing to and fro, and each arrival was greeted with cries. By craning her neck Louise was sure she saw the startling yellow of Derek's craft. It was impossible to signal to him, they were so hemmed in.

'What is it?' Louise now cried, with worry of her own.

David threw her a look and saw a rare sight. His sister was scared. Again he looked at Sam, who translated accurately.

'Don't fret, missus!' he shouted at her. 'There has obviously been some kind of problem. Your son and his wife will show up soon!'

People were assisted from a small boat and helped onto the quay. They were soaked to the skin, frightened and helpless, and in great shock. Others gathered around immediately, with blankets and mugs of hot drinks.

Louise saw medical people trying to push their way through, then another small boat arrived with more bedraggled people.

'What is it?' Louise cried. 'I must, MUST know!' and for the very first time in her life her voice cracked with hysteria. 'David! Sam! Do something! Don't just stand there! Find out!' and her voice now screeched her anguish.

David had developed a sharp, nasty gut feeling. A look over at Sam showed his thoughts were the same. He stretched forward and snatched the arm of a man being helped to one side by a nurse. 'What the hell's happened!' he roared.

The middle-aged man halted, threw a look at him, noted the female companion and shook his head sadly.

'It was thick fog and the fool captain was sailing at top speed. He must have realised at the last minute, because we turned to starboard, but it was too late. I was out on deck and suddenly a huge rock towered above us—we struck near the Casquets,' he panted with emotion. 'The steamer had no chance at all. She was doomed to go down. God help those in the engine room. They had no chance at all. I happened to look at my pocket watch. Twelve minutes from start to finish, and the *Stella* went below the waves.'

They were deeply shocked and David spoke

for them all. 'Panic?'

'None at all, and the crew were very good. They assured the passengers who'd streamed up from the salon that they'd get them all away, and they did their best. I must hand it to them. They managed to launch six boats before the *Stella* just went below the waves. It was—hell on earth!'

The man shivered with reaction. 'Come, mister. You must get to hospital!' the nurse cried.

David, Sam and Louise were rooted as people thronged around them, calling out names, trying to find their loved ones. Who had been lucky enough to get on one of the six lifeboats? How many people were still in the sea? They were all islanders and knew the dragging, suction power of a sinking ship.

David frowned at Sam and with a facial gesture indicated he was to stay with Louise. Then he roughly pushed his way through the milling people. Manners were not the order of this awful day. It was practicalities that were. He barged forward and beside a man with a clipboard who, harassed and upset, was writing down names.

'Philip and Jean Noyen. Have they landed?' he asked.

The man scanned a short list and gravely shook his head. 'Afraid not, but people are struggling ashore from other boats. The dead ones so far, they're being taken over there for formal identification,' and he pointed. 'You know these Noyens?'

David caught his breath with fresh anxiety. 'Not for half a year,' he had to admit slowly.

'Should be with a next of kin for the inquest to come, sir,' he pointed out, and nodded in the direction of Louise, who stood frozen with distress.

'Philip Noyen's mother,' David explained heavily.

The man pulled a face. 'That's a bad one,' he admitted. 'No one else, sir? There are also the bodies, though I must warn you some may not be pretty to view. The rocks.'

David groaned. He must save Louise from that and flashed a look at Sam, who caught it and realised something had to be said to him out of Louise's hearing.

'Missus, come with me. Someone is dishing out tea over there, if I'm not mistaken, and you can sit on that bollard so I can help your brother!'

Without giving her pause to think, let alone argue, he forcefully pulled Louise forward, elbowing a path for both of them, amid angry glares that he ignored. He gesticulated, pushed her onto a newly vacated bollard, while someone thrust a mug of hot tea in her hands. Then without pause he whipped around and shoved his way back to David Penford.

David explained the new situation. Sam did not hesitate. 'I can do the identifying if it becomes necessary. I know them both very well. Save the missus, but perhaps there is hope?'

David gritted his teeth. 'I have a bad feeling about this one,' he said slowly. 'Managed to grab a few words with a crewman. There were over 174 passengers and crew on the steamer, and only six boats managed to get away before she foundered. They're predicting a heavy loss of life,' he added.

'But what the devil happened?'

'From what I've managed to pick up from overheard snippets that fool captain was racing at nineteen knots—in a thick fog and in these dangerous waters. He steered to starboard much too late!' David growled.

'Deserves to be hung!' and Sam swore lustily.

'No chance of that. I heard the last seen of him was on the bridge and he went down with his ship!' David added.

'And I heard another great tale of bravery. A female stewardess, name of Mary Ann Rogers, had a lifebelt and a place in one of the boats, but she handed it and her seat over to a passenger. She's not been seen and it's feared she's gone down also,' Sam told him.

'If there are many bodies, as I think there will be, it's going to take considerable time to get them all out of the sea and bring them ashore. My sister won't leave until she knows what has happened to her son and his wife,'

David said with a groan.

Sam pulled a face, at a loss as to what to suggest. He agreed his missus would not budge an inch until she knew about Philip and Jean, even if it meant staying there for hours. 'Don't know what to suggest,' he groaned.

'Neither do I,' David replied, shaking his head and discreetly trying to keep an eye on his sister. Dear God, she did not deserve anything else bad happening to her. Not after what life has already hurled at her. 'Her grandchildren?' he asked, suddenly remembering them.

'Don't fret about them, sir. My wife and her sister will be in charge,' Sam assured him.

'What do we do now?' David asked helplessly.

Louise perched on the wharf bollard, surrounded by upset, shocked, distressed people, many in tears, men as well as women. For a few minutes she had felt herself clam up like a cold stone statue, but now she had regained control with her incredible inner strength.

She was well aware that David and Sam had excluded her deliberately from their conversation, and she now knew why. She had listened intently to the many conversations around, the predicted huge loss of life. She had overheard two rescued crew members swearing at the captain, his insane speed in the fog and in Channel Island waters. There was a huge number of passengers aboard, far more than normal because of Easter. One crewman had estimated the loss of life would top one hundred.

Without stirring she knew her son was gone from her. Why did she have to live with all these horrors? Other people did not. What did fate or destiny have against her? Her mind went back to dear Jack's death, such a huge struggle to accept. She had told herself the worst had now happened to her. Nothing more could. How foolish she had been. Had fate overheard?

She saw Sam walk aside to a building, vanish for a short while then return to David with a nod. Her instinct now told her Philip's and Jean's bodies had been recovered and were inside. Sam had been to identify.

Louise stood and walked over to them. 'It's all right,' she said with a great sigh. 'They've been found and you have done the necessary, Sam. Thank you, but he *is* my flesh and blood. I must go too.'

'No, missus!' Sam cried with alarm, and David grabbed her arm. 'Don't go. Remember them as they were—like you did with Simon!' he cried with a flash of inspiration. 'The sharp rocks. The waves and currents!'

'He's right, missus. I'm sorry to say, it's them!' Sam confirmed sadly.

Louise paused uncertainly. She suddenly realised many would wait days, perhaps even weeks, to receive a body to identify. It all depended on the whims of the sea. If this had to happen, her waiting had been short. She looked at both of her men, nodded, wiped the tears from her cheeks and turned to Sam.

'In that case, Sam, take us home please, and tomorrow arrange for me to see George Falla!'

David nodded. He knew of her need once again for her advocate. He must phone his wife and explain what had happened. When he would get home now would depend on when a steamer could arrive. Perhaps it was just as well he would be with Louise at this time. The thought of her alone with her daughter made him shake his head.

Sam ploughed a path forwards towards where he'd left the horse and cart in a side street. Distressed people reluctantly yielded a path for the three of them. Home to Cobo.

ELEVEN

Christine hurried back home, eager to see Jean. Philip was all right, but his wife was more important. She was happy to discuss fashion with her sister-in-law, who had a good eye for colour apropos of age group. That was her mother's trouble. She went around, dressed in clothes out of fashion by at least ten years, usually drab browns or greys. She was a walking disaster area for someone ambitious like her daughter. Also, Christine reflected, she could put her slight problem before Jean for her advice. There was no hurry, of course, and it might even be too trivial for serious comment. Time would tell.

She had heard about the steamer's sinking, but ships that sank were commonplace around the Channel Islands, always had been, always would.

It dawned on her that her obnoxious Uncle David would still be there—someone she disliked, and who had the same feelings for her.

'Jean?' she asked as she stepped into the large kitchen and eyed her mother. She had been—crying!

'What's the matter with you?' David snapped at her. 'Are you the only person on the entire island who hasn't heard what happened, or are you so wrapped up in yourself you don't give a damn?'

No one, especially this selfish female, was going to give more distress to his adored sister Louise. Why had it taken him so long to realise this, he asked himself angrily?

'Your brother and his wife are both dead. Drowned in the wreck of the steamer!'

'Dead?' Christine cried, as shocked as when her father went so suddenly. 'Dead?' she parroted helplessly, as she turned on her heel and went up to her room. This took some thinking about and, at the same time, its implications entered her head. It meant her mother would now bring up two grandchildren. Brats around all the time. Into everything. No privacy. Dreadful. She knew what a noisy child she had been. Once when her mother was not around she had wandered into her little private office. It was a boring, drab room like its owner. Desk, chair, shelves with uninteresting books, two pictures not particularly good in her opinion, piles of papers on the desk, covered with figures, which she had stirred with one finger just as her mother had entered.

Her mother had exploded with extreme wrath, boxed her ears, dragged her away, then threw her from the room with dire threats should this happen again. That very day Sam had examined the door and, within an hour, a locksmith had arrived and it was impossible to enter without a key. Who would really want to go back in there anyhow?

But if grandchildren were going to live here—she shook her head. This meant she would have to try and find somewhere to live. She knew she was well thought of with fashion ideas so her wages could go up accordingly, or she would work for someone else.

The next deep thought was that her brother and his Jean were dead. Drowned and probably battered by the rocks. She shivered. No one deserved to die like that. Not even miserable Uncle David.

David meanwhile was asked to respond to a knock at the door. 'Please see to it, David,' Louise asked him wearily.

He strode down the short hall, anything to help marvellous Louise. As the door opened George Falla walked in, without breaking step.

David went stiff and whipped around to protect Louise. He did not know this man and felt his hackles rise at the familiarity he showed. He opened his mouth to bellow, but the man beat him to it. He was in the kitchen and grabbed Louise in his arms and started to soothe her as of familial right.

'Shush, shush, dear niece!' he crooned. 'I'll take over, but you'll have to come to my office. Can you manage it in the morning?' he asked in a soft voice.

David stood bewildered. Niece? Uncle? Who and what the hell . . .?

The advocate looked over at him as he kept Louise in his arms, stroking her hair and forehead, hugging her tightly, then wiping her tears with a huge soft white handkerchief.

'I'm Falla, advocate, and I adopted your sister as my niece a while ago,' he explained bluntly.

David let out a sigh. 'Penford, her brother—supposed to sail back on the *Stella*,' he explained.

'Bring her to my office in the morning for ten o'clock,' George ordered sharply, 'and look

213

after her—she's still in shock!' he said coldly. He knew nothing about this brother and was prepared to be ungracious, almost without reason, because of this latest horror, and how he knew it would affect someone for whom he had the utmost admiration.

He stopped at the open door and looked sternly at the other. 'Do not allow anyone, and I mean *anyone*, to upset her!'

David recognised a harsh order when he heard one. This man was his own height and weight, though a few years older, but he had a presence about him. Then, David reminded himself, if he was an advocate in their States of Deliberation he would have heard it all before and dealt with it. Nothing would ever throw this man. He would be a powerful ally and a devilish enemy. Rather like Louise herself.

'Yes sir!' he found himself saying, words he couldn't remember last using. 'Thank God you're with my sister. I thank you, sir, for when I'm back in England. Difficult for me to get over often, even though my three girls are married and no longer underfoot,' he explained. He dived into a pocket, removed his diary, scribbled and ripped out a page and passed it over. 'My phone number!'

George Falla took it and with equal gravity placed it inside his own pocket diary. 'If I do ever call, come!' Then he nodded up the stairs. 'And watch that young missy,' he added acidly. 'She's going to give her mother grief at some

214

point!' and this was a warning David well understood. Christine was a selfish pain in anyone's backside.

The next morning he took her into the advocate's office, holding her arm comfortingly. The advocate came out, gave her a quick peck on the cheek and eyed her brother. He pointed to a seat.

'You wait here!' George stated and noted the frown on Penford's face. 'She'll be quite safe with me,' he said acidly. 'Client confidentiality!'

David did not like it, he felt so protective towards his sister, but this man was tough and faced him challengingly. 'Yes sir!' he ground out and, under his breath, muttered to himself, 'No sir and three bags full sir!'

Louise entered his familiar office and slumped in her usual chair. 'I feel washed out,' she began. 'Rather like something the cat has dragged in!'

'Perfectly understandable,' he tried to placate.

'Why always me? Why does it all happen to me?' she almost wailed. 'No one else on this island has to go through so much!'

'You asked me that once before and I told you I was not wise enough to give a sensible reply,' he said carefully.

She was emotionally wound up, as tight as a spring ready to uncoil. Louise looked at him miserably. 'They were so young!'

'And so were many others!' he replied quietly. 'Those whom the gods would destroy they first drive mad. Euripides, 484 BC, if I remember correctly, but they're not going to destroy you. You're going to be another phoenix rising from the ashes.'

Louise gave a huge sigh.'I'd like to think so,' she said unhappily. 'But I just cannot, now!'

'Of course not. It's too new, too raw, too sudden and too unexpected!'

'Oh, Uncle George!'

'You may not believe me but you *will* rise again. You have to. You have two grandsons left parentless,' he said in a soft voice. 'And you have to tell them!' he warned.

Louise nodded. 'Duret will be too young to understand. Charles is another matter. I have been pondering how to do it and thought I'd just say they have had to go away for a bit. When Charles questions, as he will, I'll keep it all very light. Not make a big issue of it. He is a typical energetic boy with lots of interests,' she explained

'Good! Encourage these. With luck, over time, he'll accept their absence, and when old enough to understand you can go into details. The other boy?'

'Too young for me yet to work out his character, but I have a feeling he is maybe a dreamer.'

'Let him dream,' George said firmly. 'Now let's deal with practicalities. I don't suppose

216

for an instant either of them were testate, and also what about the other grandparents?'

'They're older than me, a bit on the frail side, in ill health. I thought I'd make a point of Sam driving them over there one day a week. They could have them all day, which I suspect will be as much as they can cope with. Especially Charles!'

'So many people live without making a will—it's madness. Even old people, who should know better. They seem to think drawing up a will encourages death itself!'

'What do we do then?'

'The law copes with such a situation with 'inheritance rules'. The estates of the deceased couple will go for their offspring to a trust fund. However, if you're going to rear them you would be entitled to put in a claim for expenses against the trust!'

'Good God, never!' Louise cried deeply shocked. 'They are my flesh and blood. I'll rear and educate them to the best of my ability, George!' she said strongly. 'They can inherit the trust fund monies when they come of age, equally divided, and, heaven forbid, if one should die before the other, then all to the survivor!'

He had not expected anything else. 'Right. Leave all this with me. Did they have their own house or rent?'

'They were buying their own place with a mortgage.'

'Put it on the market. Empty it first, of course, and that money can kick off the trust fund,' he explained. 'All quite legitimate!' And she would have little time to brood and wallow in self-pity. 'Have you thought about your quarry monies now? Will you wish to have more cash to hand?'

Louise had not thought that far down this particular road. She did some swift mental calculations. 'Let things stay as they are. Once they get into higher education I can review the savings account,' she commented thoughtfully.

He nodded his approval once more. She was doing fine. Thinking straight. 'The quarry income is certainly excellent, and with the interest rates I managed to negotiate we're both doing quite nicely, Louise!'

He smiled at her. 'Your brother will be wondering about all this!'

'None of his business,' she said tartly. 'I don't ask him questions about his private financial affairs, and he won't ask me in case I bite back!'

'I've been asking around about this steamer. Shipwrecks and lives lost at sea are so commonplace in this bailiwick, whether it be here, Herm, Alderney, Sark, they do not even draw comment. This though is very different indeed.'

He stood, as did Louise, presuming he had another client due. He waved at her to sit as he opened the door. 'Penford! Here!' he barked.

218

David jumped then glared at him. Who the hell did this bloke think he was?

'Don't glare at me! Sit with your sister while I give you some facts I've acquired about that sinking, though some are not pretty'

He had made some discreet phone calls to English contacts, and had found Penford passed muster, was highly thought of in finance.

He paused to collect his thoughts, just checking his notepad on his desk.

'I'll give some technical details I've acquired. Help to make a better picture. The *Stella* was of the Frederika class, built on Clydebank in 1890, with a gross tonnage of 1,059 tons. She was equipped with twin screws quite capable of a top speed of nineteen knots, which can never be called exactly hanging about. She was fast.'

He paused to let them assimilate these basic facts before continuing. 'They are still finding bodies and a number of boats are bringing them ashore.'

'This is too dreadful to try and understand . . . if we had not been there!' Louise said heavily.

'The loss of life must be huge,' David said sadly.

George nodded. 'As far as I can find out, right now, there were 43 crew onboard, and 174 passengers.'

David pulled a face. 'Overloaded?' he

219

asked.

George gave him a nod. 'I think you're very right,' he told them soberly. 'They are talking of over one hundred lives lost. But if people boarded at the last moment the passenger manifest could be wrong. Speeding.'

'What!' brother and sister asked as one.

'Looks like it,' and George turned to David. 'You use the crossing a fair bit. You can imagine the situation. Two steamers, avid for trade, race each other over here. The first in grabs the best berth and the bulk of the passengers, then is off with minimum harbour dues to pay!'

'But in fog?' Louise protested.

'And the dangerous coastline of the Channel Islands in general!' David echoed his disgust and outrage.

'You're right, Penford, and I predict this disaster will bring about some long-overdue changes. There will be a court of enquiry with a Board of Trade report. Some who survived say she went down in a bare eight minutes. Others make it ten. Whatever, the crew did well to manage to launch six lifeboats, but a pitiful number for all those onboard. Great bravery too by some.'

'I heard about a female stewardess who had a place in a lifeboat with a lifebelt, but she gave up both to a passenger,' David said slowly.

George nodded. 'I too have heard that. It

was Mary Ann Rogers, and no, she has not made it. The irony of this is that she lost her husband sixteen years earlier to the same shipping company!'

'At top speed though!' Louise murmured with disbelief. 'And in a thick fog. Was the captain mad?'

George shook his head. 'That will never be known. He was at his bridge when she struck and made no attempt to save himself. He went down with her. One passenger, very much alert, states he saw a huge rock loom up suddenly, the steamer turned quickly to starboard but all much too late. She was hemmed in by rocks, grazed one, then careered over a submerged one before she could be stopped. She must have torn out her bottom as she then went down so quickly. When are you planning to return, Penford? They'll get another steamer here as soon as possible.'

David hesitated. 'I'd planned to be home for the Easter weekend, but . . .' and he shrugged his shoulders helplessly and looked firmly at the other man, as if asking a silent question. Louise saw and interpreted it.

'You must go, David. I'll be all right. I have Sam and Uncle George!'

'That's as maybe, but what about that girl of yours?' David asked dubiously.

Now Louise managed a wan smile. 'Don't think about her. Once she realises young

221

children will be around permanently I have a suspicion she'll take herself off to some place of her own, and the sooner the better as far as I'm concerned. She's become too much like hard work, and I think I'll have hands full until all settles down again—if ever!' she added heavily.

'Well?' David started uncertainly.

'No! Go! Just as soon as another ship comes in. It won't take long.'

'She's right,' George said firmly. 'And I'll be holding a very careful watching brief, Penford! You have my undertaking on that!'

David felt relief, smiled wanly at his sister, held and squeezed her hand and even smiled at the advocate. 'I'll go just as soon as possible!' he confirmed. Then he grinned. 'I think you'll do—Uncle George!'

George Falla let out one of his bellowing laughs. 'All right, you two. Clear off back to Cobo,' and he escorted them from the room and outside to where the pony and trap waited.

As soon as they arrived back Sam met them. 'Sir!' he called to David. 'I've just picked up information—another steamer will come in during the morning!'

Louise nodded. 'Take it and go, bro. Sam, drive my brother down first thing in the morning. You may have to hang about a bit, David, but it's safer to get you home for Easter!' and she noted his frown and hesitation. 'Don't fret about me. I'll be looked after and I will overcome—again,' she vowed through clenched teeth. 'Then, Sam, we must all put our heads together regarding my grandsons. Charles will be the one to ask questions. No lying. No fairy stories either. We do not know where their parents are nor when we will see them again. Back at school after Easter, Charles is going to pick up the whole story, so tell him the facts—he's old enough to understand. He won't be the only child so afflicted. Duret will just copy his brother. The thing is to keep Charles fully occupied when not at school. I think if you can get a tiny saddle he could start riding on our pony, and Sam, if you would not mind initially, it could help if you took him around with you and explained what you do and why.'

'Of course, missus,' Sam replied instantly. 'It'll be my pleasure.'

David went into his wallet, threw a look at Louise, who tactfully moved back to the house, mind whirling with what now had to be done with two youngsters permanently living with her.

David carefully handed over four crisp English five-pound notes. Sam was taken aback.

'That's nice of you, sir, but unnecessary!' he protested, pushing the generous money back.

David returned it. 'Don't argue, Sam. It is my express wish, so shut up, man!'

Sam graciously took what was, to him, a

considerable fortune, and carefully tucked it into his almost permanently empty wallet—certainly when it came to valuable English money. He nodded, threw a smile then walked away embarrassed.

The next morning Louise saw him off. 'Try to come over more often, bro!'

'I will!' he promised, and meant it.

Louise went back to planning which rooms for the grandsons, and the general rearrangement of domestic duties. She was astonished when Sam returned in no time at all. *Now* what had gone wrong, she groaned?

Sam came into her office and beamed. 'That was almost too easy, missus,' he told her. 'We'd only just arrived when a very small steamer came to take England-bound passengers. Your brother was just about the first up the gangway,' he grinned. 'I think if any man had tried to stop him he would have been flattened!'

'Splendid. Now there's going to be a lot to do. We must go through Philip and Jean's goods and chattels, see if her parents want anything, clean up that cottage and get it sold. The monies can then be invested for the grandchildren. At the same time, this weekend is Easter. We must make some kind of game hunting for little eggs for the children, but not so hard that Duret can't find one. I cannot allow two brothers to grow up disliking each other for anything, especially jealousy. Me

224

and Simon had a pretty rough childhood, because David was quite obnoxious, a bully. Until I swiped him one!' and she grinned at the memory. 'Even then, it's taken us years, decades even, to understand each other and become as close as we are today. You probably didn't have to go through this.'

Sam pulled a face. 'I just wasn't wanted at all by anyone. Best thing ever happened to me was when the advocate's mare jammed a stone in her shoe and Mr Falla was clueless at getting it out. Best day of my life,' he confided.

So she was kept busy, aided and abetted by Sam. She thus could have little time to brood about her latest tragedies, which Sam knew was good. He had seen the advocate privately and understood this man, agreeing with all that had to happen. George Falla demanded many answers to legal questions, and there were the usual Benson's board meetings and discussions. Louise was given no time at all to brood at these latest deaths.

Except at bedtime, and every night was the same. She would try and compose herself for sleep, but try as she might her departed loved ones would come into her mind. Philip and Jean, darling Jack. Gentle Simon, then her magnificent father. Every evening she would scream silently, 'Why me?' It was so horribly, cruelly unfair, then she would hear her Uncle George's calm voice telling her he was not wise enough to answer.

The first day back at school was a bad one. Charles returned with Polly, sobbing out his heart. 'It's my mum and dad. They are drowned dead!'

It had taken care and many cuddles to dry his tears, because Duret promptly copied without understanding why. Very slowly the two little boys did understand that something awful had happened with a ship. They would never see their parents ever again, but they had a wonderful grandma instead. It had been a hard time but young children are resilient, Louise told herself. At the end of that first difficult week a peaceful life had been established, which the children accepted. Louise just counted her blessings in that they had not been older and more difficult to placate.

Then there was Christine. She did not like the boys roaming upstairs and into her room, so Louise had a quiet word with Sam who fitted a bolt to the top of the door of her room. She could reach. The boys could not.

Christine was also a puzzle. She came and went with her usual sparse conversation, but twice Louise had thought her daughter wished to speak with her. Always there had been someone else present.

Louise mulled over what to do, then decided grabbing the bull by its horns was perhaps the best tactic. One evening, when she had heard Christine go to her room, and while the boys were being put to bed, she went upstairs and rapped on the bedroom door.

Christine opened and jumped when she saw her mother, then realised this was the perfect God-given time.

'Have you been trying to speak to me?' Louise asked stiffly.

'Yes, Ma, I have!' and Christine tried to marshal sensible words. She had rehearsed the speech to herself many times lately, but now the words had fled.

'I'm pregnant!' she blurted out, and stood awaiting the storm, though hoping perhaps there might be help. If only Jean had been available.

Louise stood frozen. The words had registered, but not yet quite sunk in. She was horrified, yet not surprised.

'So?' she asked acidly.

Now it was Christine's turn to be flatfooted and speechless.

Louise realised this. 'You'd better get yourself married quickly, before you start to show too much, girl!'

Christine took a deep breath. 'I can't—he *is* married!' she whispered miserably.

'You stupid girl!' Louise shouted angrily. 'What's his name? I demand to know!'

'Le Page!'

It was a common island name all through the bailiwick as well as Jersey. Louise's face had become an implacable mask of rage.

227

'It's Michael le Page, married to Lisa Domaille!'

Louise frowned. She knew a number of le Pages but not this pair. 'From where?' she barked angrily.

'Jersey!' Christine whispered, deeply frightened at the look on her mother's face. It had changed from anger and disgust to something quite terrifying.

'Jersey!' Louise bellowed. 'If you must go around dropping your knickers so easily you could, at least, have picked a Guernsey donkey, not a rotten Jersey crapaud!'

Christine backed a step. She had seen her mother angry before, but this rage was just about feral. She felt fear. Why such hatred for Jersey? Was there something in the past she had no knowledge of? Now was certainly not the time for questions. She knew her mother set great store by their worthy family name and its respectability.

Louise struggled to control her rage. She itched to lash out at this stupid girl of hers but, with an effort, she made herself consider the practicalities.

'How many months gone are you?'

Christine wished she were a thousand miles away. 'Five, Ma!' 'What?' Louise gasped, waving a hand.

Christine stood and pulled aside a long flowing top blouse and a skirt full enough to hide her belly. Louise knew the girl was very correct. Why hadn't she known about this before, she asked herself angrily? Then she answered her own question. She had rarely seen her daughter up close because Christine kept herself very much to herself. And, Louise added, her mind had always been filled with other matters. She cursed her failing and strode backwards and forwards three paces across the room, thinking at top speed.

'You can stay here until near your confinement, then off to Jersey you go. You're finished on this island. No one will ever employ or even associate with a whore,' she stated brutally.

Christine flinched but had learned only today that this was so. The fashion house had made the discovery and she was well and truly out with scathing words to boot.

'But what shall I do with myself all day in this place?' she asked with rising panic.

Louise saw her point and chewed her bottom lip. 'You can go out on our land twice a day for exercise, but not when visitors are here. At all other times you are confined to your room. As to doing what?' She paused but now had started to think logically. 'I know nothing about fashion. Not interested at all. I dress for comfort only. I will get you some big notepads so you could work designing in your room. I presume you have knowledge of colours and various textiles!'

Christine brightened. Why hadn't she

thought of that? It was a splendid and attractive idea to pass the time for another four months.

'That would be great, Ma!' she said and even managed a wan smile.

'That's that sorted then, but afterwards, you and the child get yourselves to Jersey and make a fresh life and try and concentrate on keeping your knickers up—tight!' She left the room and managed not to slam the door with her anger.

That night she slept better and realised it was rage that had exhausted her this time, and not thinking of all her dear departed. Another visit to Uncle George became necessary. She would tell David in due course, but only after talking to Uncle George. Michael le Page married to Lisa Domaille. Who was he? What was his background? She had blind faith that George Falla would have contacts on that island. It seemed that lawyers lived in tight circles where distance was no object.

A few days later George eyed her in his office. She was bubbling with anger as she explained her current situation. He must be careful how he handled her today.

'So you're going to end up with three grandchildren,' he said carefully.

'Like hell I am!' Louise snapped lustily. 'I have two only, never three, especially a bastard with Jersey blood!'

'Not all Jersey people are rogues,' he said

quietly. 'The majority are very decent people, quite a few I call friends,' he tried again.

'That's your bad luck, Uncle George!'

'Now Louise, stop it,' and he added a bark to his tone.

'I mean what I say. I have not and never will have a bastard grandson. You don't know what it's like to have a miserable childhood. Children can be very cruel little creatures at times. If one of their peers is at all different they turn and make the outsider's life hell. I can see when Charles and Duret reach a certain age and find out their half-sibling is different to them . . .' and she shook her head. 'Me and Simon had a rotten time because David was horrible, until I was big enough to stand up to him. I detested him for years, what with mother dancing attendance on him as firstborn. No. I have two grandchildren only to rear and that is very final indeed. Christine can get herself out of this mess and onto Jersey.'

He gave a heavy sigh. He could see her point and did agree with her but had no intention of saying so. 'I'll make a few enquiries. Call to see me in a week's time.' He stood, terminating the visit. 'Damn fool girl that Christine,' he thought as he saw Louise out.

Louise sat on her trike. It was too soon to go home. She had not seen Derek for a long time, so she pedalled down to the harbour, parked and walked slowly along the harbour edge,

231

peering down. She spotted a fishing smack, a vivid yellow, and could just make out the name 'Susan', and she smiled. No one else would use that colour!'

'Oi! You!'

She halted, turned and frowned. It was a disreputable fisherman who seemed a little familiar. Old, bent and filthy dirty.

'What's this I've heard about your girl dropping her knickers for my nephew?'

Louise froze at words that echoed some of hers of only a short while ago. It was in order for her to use them, but no one else. Then full recognition dawned. It was that odious Silas Regnald. Her jaw clamped like a vice. Her eyes went to narrow flares of vicious rage. The man shuddered. His big mouth! And against her! Ye gods, she was more like her old man than ever. She was—his double.

Louise took just half a step forward, balled her right fist and let fly. She was totally ignorant of boxing or pugilism but she had luck. She was strong, healthy, tall, and her fist hit Regnald on the point of the jaw. There was instant action. His eyes and mouth opened wide with pain and shock. He flung up his arms, staggered then lost his balance and fell over the harbour into the sea.

'You! I saw that. I'm going to arrest you. He'll drown,' and the shocked parish constable threw down a nearby lifebelt. Derek came on deck, saw it all and grabbed the floundering man by his collar and roughly hauled him up the ladder back onto the harbour.

'Rubbish,' Derek snapped and turned to Louise. 'You all right, madam?' he asked anxiously, ready to take on the whole of the police force for her.

'I'm fine, so yes, Constable. Go ahead and arrest me. Let me have my day in court. I promise you I'll then open my mouth, long, loud, wide and very clear!' she growled, eyes flaming wrath.

The Jersey man flinched, unable to meet those fiery eyes, and he cursed himself. She would, too, and what would happen to him? He would end up the laughing stock of Jersey, Guernsey, Alderney, Sark and Herm—just to start with. His life would be total misery. He took a deep breath and knew there was only one thing to do—apart from never tangling with Penford's girl ever again.

'I refuse to press charges or confirm anything ever happened,' he growled, and the constable saw he meant this. He glowered at the three of them, gave a deep sniff and stormed away, muttering under his breath.

Derek took the other by one sodden arm. 'Clear off, you!' he growled. 'Get back to your own island and stay there. We don't want the likes of you here—ever again. Got it?'

Silas Regnald had. He threw the other's arm off then stumbling a little, still a bit dazed, he headed back to where a little skiff

233

had brought him over from St Helier. To hell
with Guernsey. It was a dead and alive hole
anyhow. Not a patch on the more vibrant
Jersey.

TWELVE

Christine pondered. Should she tell her secret?
What was the point really? It would all come
out in due course, and she was pleased to find
she was unconcerned personally. At least she
was seeing more of her mother nowadays,
always in the evenings when the youngsters
were going to bed. Really it had turned into a
good summer. A few months ago this would
have been considered impossible. She also
enjoyed her walks when no one was around,
except Sam, and she always went out of her
way to exchange a few words with him. He was
a nice man. Why hadn't she seen this before?
There was so much that confused her, and
had done so since that awful day when her
father had died so suddenly. She admitted her
conduct had been hateful, but why she did not
know. Neither did she really care now. Why
should she with this secret?

'Oh Ma, look at this!' and she thrust her
sketchpad forward. 'You use your trike a
lot, so how about this for a divided skirt with
pockets both sides! And it should be a darkish

green with tan facings.'

Louise studied the sketch gravely, and her eyebrows shot up. 'This is good, really good. I like it!' She was really impressed. The girl did have talent and a flair for design. This should stand her in good stead when she made a new life for herself on the other island. 'I'll see about getting this made up right away,' she promised.

Christine was delighted and also satisfied. They exchanged quite warm smiles, which promised a new beginning.

Louise watched her daughter carefully and suspected she was more advanced than either she or the doctor thought. She intended to mention this to George at her next visit, but he just opened his office door to her, pointed to her chair and barked, 'Sit!'

Taken aback, she did.

'What's this I hear about you brawling in public?' he asked sternly.

'Oh that!' Louise grinned.

Then he had to remove his cold features and break into laughter. 'I'd like to have seen it!' he chortled.

'Well it shut him up, and I think for good. Hopefully!' she added. 'Have you obtained any information, George?'

'Some! Michael le Page works at the market over there, when sober that is. It appears he's a handsome bloke to females and has the charm to bewitch them. The person to be sorry for is

235

his long-suffering wife. She never really knows whether she'll get the housekeeping before he drinks it away. No children, so she would be an ideal person to adopt if Christine is willing to let the baby go,' he added soberly.

Louise nodded thoughtfully. 'Nothing can be done right now, but I think my girl is more advanced than either she or her doctor says. I know better than to go and question. Patient confidentiality,' she paused, almost dramatically.

'And you, Louise?' he asked, gentle with her now.

She pulled a face and gave a huge sigh. 'Will my life ever be normal again?'

'It will. I promise!' he told her and took one of her hands in his. 'But even if more blows are to come for you, you'll always be Danny's girl. Remember his favourite saying?'

She smiled. 'There is nothing more certain than . . .!' ' . . . life is uncertain!' he finished for her.

'Oh well, George. I'd better get back,' she said, standing. 'My trike's outside. No time to cycle down and see Derek. Do you know I believe he was ready to flatten Regnald and even the parish constable. What true loyalty! I *am* lucky!'

*   *   *

She was tested yet again. On her return Polly

236

met her. 'Sam

has taken your daughter into the doctor then on to the hospital. I think that baby is coming. She started with pains all of a sudden!'

'So soon!' Louise gasped with shock.

'Here, missus. Sam is back!' Polly cried and pointed.

Sam bounded up the stairs and into the hall. 'The pony is still outside, missus. Let's get you to the hospital. This is one baby in a tearing hurry to arrive!' he gasped red-faced with exertion and stress.

Louise hastened to follow him, suddenly confused and worried. This was not going at all as a normal pregnancy. They had no word as Sam drove fast, even recklessly, to the little hospital. He helped her alight then led the way inside.

'Delivery room, name of Noyen!' he shouted.

'Sit over there and wait,' a nurse told them briskly.

Louise and Sam sat side by side. Neither had words. Both felt a drama was being played out and they were helpless. Quite useless.

'Oh Sam!' Louise said in a low voice. Her inside was in turmoil, and she had a dreadful, quite frightening feeling without understanding why. He could only grab her hand and hold it with sympathy.

They sat seemingly endlessly, then a baby's cries reached them. Sam beamed and turned to her. 'If that's our baby there is nothing wrong with those lungs,' he chuckled.

Louise held her tongue. She and Sam didn't always have the same opinion, and her lips compressed in a tight line, which he missed.

A door opened suddenly and a doctor appeared and walked over. 'Madame Noyen?'

Louise nodded and stood as he beckoned her to a private part of the room. 'I'm sorry. I tried but it was hopeless. Did your daughter confide in you?'

Louise shook her head blankly. 'About what?'

'I understand your husband died suddenly from a heart attack. He'd had two warnings from his doctor and the third attack was fatal. Your daughter has just died from the same condition. I didn't like the sound of her heart from the start, and I warned her the stress of childbirth might prove fatal. I'm afraid I was correct. It was probably something inherited from her father. He had no idea about it either, from what your daughter told me. There is a lot we do not know about heart conditions, and little we can do. Medical science has a long way to go regarding the heart.'

'She's—dead?' Louise asked flinching.

He nodded and waited for hysterics but recognised inner strength when he saw it. 'The baby is fine. A strong, healthy boy, weighing in at seven pounds. Splendid baby!' he soothed, now deeply concerned as she just stood there, rigid, frozen, in deep shock.

Louise's mind was in turmoil. Christine had known and never said a word to her! Just sketched her new skirt! She felt a deep pang of guilt. Had the gulf between them been so enormous? If so, was it her fault? So much galloped through her mind.

'Myself and my retainer will view and identify the body,' she managed to get out slowly and heavily. 'The baby is to be kept here for the time being. Hire a wet nurse if necessary.'

'Surely you'll want to take him home?' the doctor asked, deeply puzzled at her reaction. Most females would have clamoured to take the infant with them. This Madame Noyen came from some unusual mould. It was as if she had some other plan that was beyond him.

'Very well, madam,' he managed to get out. 'For how long though?'

'You will be notified. Come, Sam. Another body to identify.'

The doctor grasped her words. Was she another who had lost loved ones in the *Stella* tragedy?'

Sam stood uncertainly, moved to her side and gave her his arm. In a solemn little procession they went into where Christine's body now lay on a bed, decently covered with a sheet to her neck. In a basinet nearby a baby lustily squalled for attention.

Louise stared and nodded slowly. 'I confirm identity!' she told her doctor in a heavy tone. This was what had never entered her head. Just as it hadn't with Jack. Sam stood rigid and nodded at the doctor.

'The name is to be Victor as a male. It was to be Victoria after the queen if a girl! She confided that much in me!' Louise said with a great sigh. She then turned to Sam. 'Drive me to George Falla's place and leave me there. I'll get a lift home myself. I've shown you how to use the telephone. Ring my brother and let him know what's happened. I'll speak to him myself this evening. He need not come over. Nothing can be done.'

Sam nodded uncertainly. He had known her for so many years now and considered he had met her every mood. Not that of right now. Her face was a cold mask of total implacability. He just did as he was ordered in silence.

George was surprised when his receptionist came and told him. This visit had to mean something more that was bad. He eyed her carefully as she sat in her chair, looking at and even through him. He said nothing. Just waited.

Louise started to speak and carefully related every word of the doctor's, then of her look at the body and the baby.

'I never expected anything like this!' George said reflectively.

'Neither did I,' Louise admitted. Her jaw

set. 'The baby is not, under any circumstances, to come to my home. That would be the thin edge of the wedge, and I do know what I'm doing!' she said and gave him a flat, almost challenging look.

This he knew was definitely not the time or place to hector. 'So what now?'

'Can you get in touch with Mrs le Page and find out quickly if she would like to adopt a healthy baby boy to be called Victor? I'll settle a sum in trust on her for the child for a few years.'

He nodded. Such practical matters were his forte, and he approved of this. It did make the perfect solution all round. 'From what my contacts have told me, le Page will never make old bones,' he told her. 'He's just too fond of the booze and this includes spirits as well from that rogue uncle of his, Silas Regnald. Mrs le Page might get great happiness from taking on a baby. She doesn't get much from that husband of hers.'

Louise frowned. 'Would the baby be safe in such a home?'

He was very sure of his facts now. 'I can just about guarantee that. If she had a baby and he made one hostile move towards it he might well end up with a carving knife in his guts one night.'

Louise gave a sigh of relief. 'Get things moving as fast as possible, George. Take monies from my savings account. Arrange for

Mrs le Page to come here and collect the baby, and no! I do not wish to meet her, and neither is she to know anything about me or anything more than basic necessities!'

'Very well, Louise. I take it you've thought this through—at such short notice. There will be no changing your mind later!' he warned her calmly.

'I know. I'm firm. It will be much better for the baby. He'll have a good life. An only child? He'll probably grow up knowing marvellous love and kindness.'

'Yes, I agree with you. People speak so highly of Mrs le Page,' he confirmed. He had, initially, been hostile to such a plan of hers, but on reflection, and after her own experiences as a girl, he was in no position to argue. His boyhood had been idyllic in comparison.

It was later on, when she finally reached home, that she put Sam totally in the picture.

'Don't agree at all, missus!' he said bluntly, from the years of working for her.

Louise was too relieved to have solved what had threatened to be a gigantic problem. 'Tough!' she snapped a little.

Sam was unused to being addressed in that tone of voice, and he had the wisdom to drop the subject. Would brother David be an ally, he wondered? Then he dismissed that idea also. He could never go behind the back of the missus. Besides, was there something in her past about which he lacked knowledge? He would never mention the subject again, he vowed, and he did not for decades.

George Falla could move fast when he had sufficient reason. That was the current situation. He called Louise to see him again then sat back in his chair, relaxed.

'So that's all dealt with. As the next of kin you signed the adoption papers and now they and the baby have gone to Jersey.'

'What is Mrs le Page like?' Louise asked anxiously. She did not want any hiccups at this late stage or another sad experience.

'A very nice lady indeed. I was dubious about the whole affair, but not anymore. To be frank, this lady will make a much better mother than ever Christine would have done. You have also acted correctly. I gave a lot of thought to your comments, but you were right. Victor le Page is going to be one very happy little boy.'

'Does Mrs le Page know the father's identity?'

'Yes, I gave it to her straight. It was the only decent thing to do, wasn't it, Louise?'

'A very remarkable person!' Louise murmured with relief. 'So perhaps I can now get on with my life and deal with two very energetic grandsons!'

'And enter your half-century year!' he joked. 'Your savings account has taken a hit recently,' he pointed out.

'That will soon recover, with the way our stone and aggregate are selling,' she told him. 'Philip and Jean's property has sold.'

'As soon as those monies come to hand I'll get them put in the trust fund. As you are the official next of kin, there'll be more papers to sign and get lodged?'

'All this legal work,' she murmured. 'I'm going home and I intend to pedal gently by the coastline. Enjoy this sunshine with, at last, a completely clear mind. Just wish Jack was with me,' she murmured wistfully as she stood.

He gave her a hug and saw her out. She mounted her trike and waved to him, and he shook his head slowly. It still astounded him how, as she became older, she even more resembled her father. Right now, standing head held high, tall, proud and sure of herself, she was the spitting image of Danny Penford. It was—uncanny.

She went down the road, parked her trike and knocked on Janet's door, which was swiftly opened. Once inside they hugged. Two old friends glad to see each other.

'I don't know what to say to you, dear Louise,' Janet told her, eyes prickling with open tears.

'Don't cry. You'll set me off,' Louise managed to get out as they sat together companionably.

'So much bad happens to you. Jack, Simon, your pa, your son and his wife, and now your daughter as well. Fate is so cruel!' Janet whispered.

'She certainly doesn't appear to like me,' Louise replied thoughtfully, and in a heavy voice, her own tears welling. 'But there are so many families now grieving on this island.'

Janet changed the subject before they both started to cry. 'I've sold out to your quarry manager's son. Young Smythe intends to make his life here and said this will be a perfect family home, and he gave me a good price. Next—me! Derek and Susan le Cromier have also purchased a new property, which has a ground-floor flat. I'm going to be their tenant at a reasonable rent as well.'

'Splendid!' Louise said, and meant it. 'All these stairs here must be too much for your knees. And they know where I live. It's a change to have some good news after . . .' and she waved a hand in the air with a symbolic gesture. 'When or whether dear Sarnia will recover from that *Stella* I don't' know. It may take years, perhaps even generations. Did you know that they think the final count of lives lost will be 105?'

'So many!' Janet murmured with sad awe.

'Not stopping long this time. If you want help moving, Sam will oblige, I know. I intend to have some exercise and fresh air and try and sort out my own mind and my losses. I have to learn to come to terms with all now I have two grandchildren to rear!'

245

'Will you be able to manage? After all, you're not young yourself anymore!'

'I'm fit, strong and, praise be, healthy. Those two scamps will also keep me young, I predict!' and she grinned.

'God bless you, dear Louise. Your pa would be so, so proud of his girl!'

So with a final hug and kiss Louise mounted her trike and prepared for a brisk ride.

She went to the south of Cobo Bay then pushed her trike, walking and looking around keenly. The tide was on the ebb, with a hint at rocks still hidden. She walked up to the promontory known as Grandes Rocques. She rested her trike and stepped onto them. When the winds came the sea would smash over her, and that would be highly dangerous.

She looked up at a dull sky, with the sun just flitting in and out almost teasingly. She opened her mouth and screamed at the rising wind.

'Jack! Simon! Pa! Philip—why have you all left me?'

Hysteria filled her voice, and tears flowed from her eyes. 'I miss you all so, so much!' she howled into the rising wind. She wiped her eyes with her hands then stumbled back down to her trike. She was NOT alone anymore. She had two splendid grandsons to rear and the family name was good, sound and respected again. She was fit, healthy and very strong physically as well as mentally. She had—

246

almost—enjoyed this wave of unusual hysteria. Now she was fit, and ready to go on again and face the world once more. Her beloved world of—Sarnia.

HISTORY

When the great liner the *Titanic* sank with that horrendous loss of life, many people in Guernsey began to refer to the sinking of the *Stella* as 'Guernsey's *Titanic.*' Well over one hundred people died, which was a huge loss of life for one little island. There were great acts of bravery and none more so than that exhibited by the stewardess Mary Ann Rogers, who had a lifebelt and her place in one of the six lifeboats. Without pause or hesitation she gave up both to a passenger. She died.

This captured the public's imagination, and a handsome drinking fountain made of stone was unveiled on 27th July 1901, opposite Southampton Pier. There was another memorial at Postman's Park to her in the City of London. In June 1997 the Board of Administration unveiled a metal plaque on the outer harbour wall at St Peter Port, in memory of all those many who perished on the *Stella*.

In June 1973 two of the Channel Islands' most experienced divers went down and found the wreck, but to stop souvenir hunters from plundering it the divers agreed to keep the location secret. A chamber pot, a ceramic tile and a small dish went on display at the Maritime Museum and Shipwreck Centre at

Bembridge on the Isle of Wight, obtained by
another diver before secrecy was imposed.

GUERNSEY'S NATIONAL ANTHEM

Sarnia; dear Homeland, Gem of the sea.
Island of beauty, my heart longs for thee.
Thy voice calls me ever, in waking, or sleep,
Till my soul cries with anguish, my eyes ache
    to weep.
In fancy I see thee, again as of yore
Thy verdure clad hills and thy wave beaten
    shore.
Thy rock sheltered bays, ah! of all thou art
    best,
I'm returning to greet thee, dear island of rest.

Chorus
Sarnia Cherie. Gem of the Sea.
Home of my childhood, my heart longs for thee.
Thy voice calls me ever, forget thee I'll never
Island of beauty. Sarnia Cherie.

I left thee in anger, I knew not thy worth
Journeyed afar, to the ends of the earth.
Was told of far countries, the heav'n of the
    bold,
Where the soil gave up diamonds, silver and
    gold.
The sun always shone, and 'race' took no part,
But thy cry always reached me, its pain
    wrenched my heart.
So I'm coming home, thou of all art the best.
Returning to greet thee, dear island of rest.

There is also a version in Guernesiais (Guernsey-French). George Deighton wrote 'Sarnia Cherie' in 1911, with Domenico Santangelo composing the tune the following year. It was first performed at St Julian's Theatre in November 1911.

ORMER CASSEROLE

Ingredients

As many ormers as possible
A strip or two of belly pork
2-3 carrots
2-3 shallots
Guernsey butter
Bay leaf
Salt and pepper

Preparation
Soak the ormers in fresh water for an hour, prize from shell. Wash, rub, trim and beat with steak hammer.

Flour ormers and brown in a frying pan with Guernsey butter. Place ormers in a casserole dish with cubes of belly pork and other ingredients. Add salt and pepper. Put in pre-heated oven at 160/170 degrees for two hours. Turn down oven and allow to simmer until cooked.

Enjoy!!!